THE HERO SHE LOVES

UNBROKEN HEROES
BOOK 5

ANNA HACKETT

The Hero She Loves

Published by Anna Hackett

Copyright 2025 by Anna Hackett

Cover by Hang Le Designs

Cover image by Wander Aguiar

Edits by Tanya Saari

ISBN (ebook): 978-1-923134-50-8

ISBN (paperback): 978-1-923134-51-5

WHAT READERS ARE SAYING ABOUT
ANNA'S ACTION ROMANCE

**The Powerbroker - Romantic Book of the Year
(Ruby) winner 2022**

**Heart of Eon - Romantic Book of the Year
(Ruby) winner 2020**

Cyborg - PRISM Award Winner 2019

**Unfathomed and Unmapped - Romantic Book
of the Year (Ruby) finalists 2018**

**Unexplored – Romantic Book of the Year
(Ruby) Novella Winner 2017**

**Return to Dark Earth – One of Library
Journal's Best E-Original Books for 2015 and
two-time SFR Galaxy Awards winner**

CHAPTER ONE

She hated waiting.

Like, really hated it.

US Marshal Jenna Sheridan tapped her boot on the tarmac. She resisted the urge to check her watch. Again.

"Why is it so cold?" Deputy Marshal Owen Briggs clunked down the steps from the private jet and joined her at the bottom.

"It's Alaska," she replied.

"But it's spring. Summer will be here soon. It shouldn't be this cold."

He stopped beside her, pulling on a navy-blue windbreaker like hers. It had *US Marshal* emblazoned on the back.

Owen had been her partner for the last eight months. He was fit and trim, with dark skin, a handsome face, and short, black hair. She'd been training him, and he had a hell of a lot of potential. He was smart, which balanced out his habit of being a little over-eager.

They were here to collect a dangerous fugitive who'd come to Alaska to hide, but had been apprehended.

Two other marshals and the Alaska State Troopers were transporting him to the jet.

She looked at her watch. They were late.

Jenna wanted Kyle Olson secured and in the air.

Her cellphone rang, and when she saw the name on the screen, she rolled her eyes. She pressed the phone to her ear. "Sheridan."

"You airborne yet?" Senior Deputy Marshal Vic McDermott's voice rang with impatience.

"No," she told her ex.

She hadn't listened to her friends, or her own intuition, and had dated a colleague. Vic had worn her down with his pursuit. She'd actually admired his tenaciousness.

She'd thought it meant he really felt something for her.

Thank God she'd never slept with him. Clearly something in her hindbrain had known something was off.

They'd dated for just over a month. Sure, Vic was arrogant, confident, and opinionated, but he was a damn good marshal. She'd thought their bond over work would make them a good team. Her work was the most important thing in her life.

But their relationship had imploded quickly. It really sucked to come home from a tough work trip transporting dangerous criminals to surprise the guy you liked...and find him in bed with his neighbors' twenty-year-old daughter.

Jenna had walked out the door and never looked back. Unfortunately, she still had to work with him.

"Get a move on, Sheridan," Vic said.

"I know how to do my job, McDermott. They haven't arrived at the plane yet."

"They're late."

Thank you, Captain Obvious. "I'll keep you posted." She ended the call.

"Must be hard working with your ex."

She shot Owen a sharp look. "He's barely an ex. It was just a couple of dinners."

The younger man held up his hands. "Sorry."

She huffed out a breath. "Learn from my mistake, Owen. It can be hard work, especially when he's an asshole."

Owen coughed, and she was pretty sure he'd mumbled something about McDermott being a major asshole.

Her lips twitched, but she refocused her gaze on the road leading into Fairbanks Airport.

No convoy in sight.

She didn't have time for Vic. He was just another reminder that men lied, and a handsome face could hide a lot of darkness.

There was no way in hell she was thinking of her father right now.

She tapped her boot again. Then she pulled her phone out and called Deputy Marshal William Lopez who was in charge of the transport. It rang and rang with no answer.

She felt a cold shiver down her spine. She was well

aware that Kyle Olson was exceptionally dangerous. And well-trained.

She tried to call Lopez again. Nothing. Next, she tried the deputy marshal who was with him. No answer.

"Fuck."

"Problem?" Owen asked, face serious.

"Neither of the marshals are answering and they're late."

Owen shrugged. "There's spotty cellphone coverage out here."

"My gut says we have a problem. Olson is dangerous."

Owen made a scoffing sound. "Maybe, but he can't take out two marshals and the two state troopers escorting them."

Owen was wrong. Olsen could easily do that.

Her phone rang. "Sheridan."

"Senior Deputy Marshal Sheridan, this is Lieutenant Dunford from Fairbanks. We have a problem."

Double fuck. Just from the serious tone of the man in charge of the local state troopers, she knew this was bad.

"We lost contact with the convoy ten minutes ago," Dunford said. "One of my troopers just managed to call. The prisoner has escaped. He crashed the vehicle he was in, and injured my men. He's escaped on foot."

Jenna closed her eyes, then opened them. "Where? We'll meet you there." She clicked her fingers at Owen. "SUV. Now."

The young marshal jogged off.

"Sheridan, I knew this fugitive was dangerous, but not this dangerous." Dunford sounded pissed. "Senior

Deputy Marshal McDermott assured us this would be a simple transport."

Well done, Vic. "Lieutenant, this fugitive is as dangerous as they get. Are your troopers okay? Where are my marshals now?" Lopez would be spitting mad. He had a fiery temper. Her mind was already focusing on where Olson would go. She started planning the search in her head.

"One of my men was injured in the crash, and the other has a bullet wound. Just a graze, thankfully." The lieutenant paused. "Sheridan, your marshals are dead."

She froze. "What?"

"I'm sorry. My man said Olson shot them both, execution style."

Static filled her ears. *Dammit, no.* Grief hit her hard. Lopez had a big family, with kids and grandkids. Deputy Marshal Calt was young. His kids were toddlers. She looked down at her boots and wrestled her emotions down. She couldn't think of them right now. "I'm on my way. Lieutenant, we need to find Olson. Fast."

"I will find him," Lieutenant Dunford said darkly. "He hurt my men, killed yours. And this is *my* state." He gave her the location.

"We're on our way." She slid the phone away just as Owen pulled up in a silver Chevy Tahoe. She climbed in.

"How bad?" Owen asked.

Jenna fought not to grind her teeth together. Leaning over, she tapped the address into the navigation system. "Lopez and Calt are dead. The troopers are both injured. Olson is in the wind."

Owen cursed. "They're dead?" His hands clenched on the wheel.

"The only way we can help them now is to find Olson."

Her partner nodded. The tires squealed as he pulled out.

Jenna sent Vic a text message. He called instantly, but she ignored him. This was partly his fault. He hadn't assigned enough resources, and he'd downplayed the risk to the troopers.

She'd warned Vic repeatedly that Olson was dangerous, and he hadn't believed her.

Kyle Olson had a special skill set. He'd just proven that.

It would take someone with the same skill set to track him down.

"We'll run this fucker down." Owen's hands flexed on the wheel. His voice was filled with the overconfidence of someone who didn't fully comprehend the situation.

"We won't. Olson's too good. He can survive in the worst terrain, and he's trained to kill."

Owen's brow creased. "You make him sound like the boogeyman."

"I'd prefer the boogeyman." She sucked in a breath. "But we *are* going to find him. We just need some help."

As they headed out of Fairbanks, Jenna scrolled through the contacts list and touched a name. The call rang, then connected.

"Norcross," a deep voice said.

"Vander, it's US Marshal Jenna Sheridan."

"Jenna, always a pleasure. What can I do for you?"

Ahead, she spotted the ruined cars in the distance. There were several Alaska State Trooper vehicles parked nearby, lights flashing. There was an ambulance, as well. The black SUV the marshals had been driving was on its roof. It looked like it had rolled several times.

Dammit.

"We apprehended Kyle Olson in Alaska," she said.

There was silence. "Good," Vander replied. "He's dangerous."

"Vander, he escaped during transport to the Fairbanks airport." The anger was building inside her, scorching hot. "He killed two of my marshals."

A curse cut across the line. "I'm sorry, Jenna."

"I need help."

HE STEPPED out of the back door of his cabin and breathed in the fresh air. Standing there for a moment, he took in the view. His cabin sat at one end of a small lake. Mountains rose up in the distance, and spring had turned everything a lush green.

Best of all, there wasn't a single person or another cabin in sight.

Parker Conroy took another step, and almost rolled an ankle on part of a pinecone.

"*Dammit.*" He picked it up. "Red, I told you to quit it."

Since he'd moved in a couple of months ago, a red squirrel had started hanging around. Red liked to leave

Park gifts of a dubious nature. Last week, it had been a ratty Barbie doll head. Park had no idea where the animal had found that.

He tossed the pinecone off the deck and heard rustling in the trees.

"I hear you. No food for you today."

Park headed to the pile of wood that he'd been chopping. It was springtime, but the nights could still get cold.

He set one log on another, then lifted the axe. He pulled in another deep breath. *Whack.*

This was a far cry from his job as a special-forces operative in Ghost Ops. After a stint in Delta Force, it had been an honor to be selected for the Ghost Ops program. The teams were made up of the best and toughest of the special forces.

He'd been sent on the most challenging and dangerous missions that existed. He'd been good at it. Thrived on it.

Until...he hadn't.

Until he'd woken up in a hospital bed, full of bullet holes and covered in burns and cuts.

The black memories crowded in, filling his head with a rush of nasty whispers. He gritted his teeth and through sheer force of will, he blocked them.

He swung the axe again. That was the past. He'd bought this old cabin in Alaska to be alone. Where it was quiet. He looked around.

Okay, sometimes a little too quiet.

But he didn't want people around, poking and talking and... No, he just wanted to be left alone.

He got busy chopping wood, and soon pulled his T-shirt off and tucked it into the back of his jeans. It wasn't long before he had a huge stack of wood. Gathering up an armload, he carried some toward the cabin. He glanced out at the lake. He might try some fishing tomorrow.

There was plenty of daylight late into the night this time of year. Even though it felt like the afternoon, it was time to make some dinner. He had a steak marinating in the fridge.

Once he'd stacked the wood, he fired up his little grill, and threw the steak on it. Back inside, he pulled out some carrots, green beans, and broccoli. He'd recently stocked up and still had fresh vegetables. Once those ran out, he'd switch to frozen and canned for a while. He chopped them up, hesitated, then sighed. He put half of the vegetables in a pot and the other half on a small plate. He carried the plate out and set it on the back steps.

As he flipped the steak, he heard a skittering sound, and a tiny, red squirrel appeared.

"Asshole," Park muttered. "I could have broken my ankle."

Red chittered at him, completely unrepentant. He snatched up a carrot, then darted across the deck.

Park served up his steak. Back in the compact kitchen with its aging cabinets and appliances, he added the vegetables. Then, he grabbed himself a bottle of beer and sat at the small, wooden table. The cabin was basic. The previous owner had left some hand-hewn furniture behind, and that was all he needed. There was a decent brown-leather sofa in the tiny living area, and a king-size bed in the only bedroom. The bathroom needed over-hauling, though. It had godawful green tiles, but a nice, wooden vanity. He'd been watching some videos online about tiling and planned to do the reno himself.

He cut some steak and ate it. This sure beat endless MREs. He hoped never to have to eat his meal out of a ration pack ever again.

As he chewed, the scars on his neck tugged. He rubbed the scar that ran along his jaw and down the side of his neck. Burn and knife scars covered parts of his right side. A souvenir from his torturers.

His gut cramped. Actually, there were a lot of things he didn't miss about the military.

He sipped his beer, then grabbed his remote and turned on the TV.

"Breaking news." An earnest young male presenter stared into the camera. "A dangerous fugitive has escaped US Marshals and Alaska State Troopers south of Fairbanks."

Park stilled. That was his neck of the woods.

"Be alert for a strange man on foot. Two marshals were killed during the escape, and troopers injured. They're currently recovering in the hospital. The fugitive is considered armed and dangerous."

The story changed, and Park cut into his steak. They hadn't shared the fugitive's name. Weird.

He flicked through channels and found a movie. It was an action flick, and as soon as he saw the way the hero held his weapon, Park rolled his eyes. He changed the channel again, and found a science fiction movie.

He took another sip of beer. This would do.

He was watching a lot more TV than he had previously. Part of it was the dead silence here in Alaska. He'd wanted solitude, and he'd gotten it, but he hadn't realized just how silent it would be. He simply wasn't used to it yet, but he'd get there.

This is what you wanted, Conroy.

As he ate, his thoughts turned to his former Ghost Ops buddy, Sawyer Lane. He wondered how Sawyer was doing. Parker had recently gone to Hawaii, where Sawyer was a deputy sheriff. He'd helped Sawyer keep his girlfriend, Hollis, safe after some asshole had put a contract out on her life.

There were some pitfalls when you fell for an A-list Hollywood actress. Still, Sawyer was smitten, and Park was happy for them.

He rubbed his scar again. He had no interest in a woman. Since his torture, he couldn't stand being touched. He tolerated handshakes and hugs with his friends, but that was about it.

The thought of anyone touching him made his muscles tense up.

Yeah, he'd recovered from his injuries, but his torture had left him fucked up in other ways. He'd spent twenty-two days in hell. Locked in a cage with the lights on, multiple men beating the shit out of him.

Now, he just wanted to be alone.

Lucky for him, there wasn't anyone around here, and definitely no women.

He sipped his beer and focused on watching the humans trying to fight off killer aliens.

Nope, there was just him, his solitude, and an annoying squirrel to keep him company. Just what he wanted.

CHAPTER TWO

P ark rhythmically hissed out breaths, doing another set of pull-ups. He'd installed the bar on the wall in the living room. He might have left the military, but he still worked out every day and kept in shape.

Sweat slid down his neck. He'd already ditched his shirt.

He planned to work on some fencing that needed replacing today. He was still doing pull-ups, pushing through the burn, when he heard the crunch of tires on the gravel out front.

He lowered his feet to the floor and frowned. He definitely wasn't expecting anyone. He barely knew anyone around here, and he was close to an hour out of Fairbanks.

Grabbing his towel, he wiped the sweat off his face and chest, then headed for the front door.

He opened it to see a silver Tahoe in front of his place. The driver's door opened, and he watched a long, denim-clad leg appear.

The woman closed the door and glanced around, watchful and alert. He didn't need to see the badge clipped to her belt to know that she was law-enforcement. A crisp, white shirt was tucked into the trim waistband of her dark jeans. She was tall, with honey-blonde hair pulled up in a ponytail.

Park felt a shot of... *Nothing.* He had no interest in a woman, no matter how attractive.

She headed toward the cabin and her gaze locked on him.

Her face was too angular to be called beautiful. Her features were too strong and bold, but she was eye-catching. He guessed she was around thirty. She walked with purpose, and kept her gaze on him, assessing. She wasn't shy.

He should have pulled on his T-shirt, but he hadn't been expecting guests. He knew his scars were hard to miss.

But as she approached, she eyed his chest and abs and he didn't see any curiosity or disgust on her face.

"You lost?" he asked.

"No. I'm Senior Deputy Marshal Jenna Sheridan."

"Well, Marshal, I've got no business with you, so get back in your SUV and go."

She stopped at the bottom step to the front deck. "You always this friendly?"

"Yes."

"I'm here to talk with you, Mr. Conroy."

Damn, she knew who he was. That didn't bode well. "I moved to Alaska so I wouldn't have to talk to anyone."

She took another step, and the breeze brought him

her scent. Like her, it was bold, and made him think of heady, lush flowers.

Flowers? Jeez. What do you care how she smells, Conroy?

"We had a dangerous fugitive escape custody yesterday," she said.

"Don't care."

She arched a brow. "You don't care that a dangerous criminal is on the loose in your area?"

Park crossed his arms over his bare chest. "No."

"He killed two marshals." Her mouth flattened and something flashed in her eyes.

Hell. Park knew how it felt to lose friends that you worked side-by-side with.

"I'm sorry," he said gruffly.

She took another step up. "I need your help to find him."

"Hell, no." He went to close the door. "You have an entire service of marshals, you don't need me."

She moved fast and jammed her boot in the door. "I do need you, Parker."

Their gazes clashed. Her eyes were blue. They had a darker rim and were paler in the center. For a second, he felt the air charge. They stared at each other, part challenge, part...something else.

He uttered a curse. "This isn't my circus."

She shoved against the door and took one step inside. "I don't believe you. I know you'd want to help stop this man."

"You don't know me."

"I know you served your country. I know that you

were a member of Ghost Ops for several years, and were damn good at it."

Park scowled. That was classified information. "It seems you know a lot about me." He didn't like it. "Then you should also know that I'm retired. I just want to live in peace and quiet."

"I know you're a man with principles, Mr. Conroy. You won't let a murderer and rapist roam the countryside."

Shit. "Rapist?"

"Yes. He likes to hurt women then shoot them between the eyes. He's well-trained. It's a miracle we caught him the first time." She looked away, her face tight.

He felt the frustration radiating off her. A part of him stirred.

No. He stomped on it. He was out. This wasn't his problem. He didn't want to get dragged back in.

"I can't help you."

She turned her head. Her blue eyes weren't cold. There was heat in them. "You're the only person who can help, Parker."

He growled. "Why? Why me?"

"Because the fugitive we're hunting is former Ghost Ops."

The news was like a punch to his gut. "What?"

She straightened. "Vander Norcross recommended you. Said you're the only person who could outthink this man and help me apprehend him."

Shit. Hell. Fuck. Park felt a storm of emotions. Vander had been one of the best commanders Ghost Ops had ever had. One of the best Parker had ever served with. He respected the hell out of Vander.

But it was the thought of this woman, Jenna Sheridan, hunting this asshole down alone that left him most unsettled.

He sighed and pushed the door open. "Come in."

JENNA SAT AT THE SCRATCHED-UP, wooden table, watching Parker Conroy making coffee.

Even without Vander telling her his past, she would've known that he had military training. The man emanated a dangerous vibe.

He was tall, lean, with black hair shaved short. He'd pulled a shirt on—unfortunately—covering the etched muscles that had been on full display earlier. The man was in top shape, with zero body fat.

The shirt also covered the scars she'd seen. They were on the right side of his torso and ran up his neck to his strong jaw. They'd looked like knife cuts and burn marks. She had no idea how he'd gotten them, but it had to have hurt like hell.

He turned and carried two mugs to the table. He shoved his chair out, the feet scraping on the floor. He sat across from her, but she felt his presence.

There were no smiles, or jokes, or fidgeting. Just a serious look on a face that was almost handsome. His mouth was a flat line and his eyes were brown. Although, that word didn't do them justice—they were a mix of dark-brown and gold. Tiger's eyes.

Once, when her father had taken her to the zoo when she was a kid, a tiger had come right up to the glass and stared at her. She'd seen its eyes, felt its intense, predatory stare. Parker Conroy had a lot in common with that tiger.

"Talk," he said.

A man of few words. Okay, so he was hot, but grouchy as hell.

Jenna didn't mind. She'd take grouchy over sleazy and insincere any day. She had to interact with federal agents and marshals like that daily. Men looking to climb the ladder by using charm and sleaze. Hell, she'd been dumb enough to date one.

She'd learned a long time ago that men only showed you what they wanted you to see. They kept their dark secrets locked up.

"The fugitive's name is Kyle Olson," she told him.

"Aw, hell." Parker sat back in his chair.

"You've heard of him."

"Yes. He's bad news."

"I know. I'm aware that he was released from Ghost Ops."

Parker made a sound. "Booted out."

"I don't know the particulars. All I got was a bunch of redacted reports, and most of it is classified."

Parker nodded. "The man liked killing, a little too much."

"Were you on the same team?"

Parker shook his head. "No, but what interaction I did have with him, I didn't like."

"After he left the military, he laid low for a while." She sipped her coffee. "He moved around a lot—Arizona,

17

New Mexico, Texas. Then, he murdered a man outside Fort Worth. It appears they got into a fight in a bar. Olson waited outside, then beat the man to death."

Parker tapped a finger on the table. "I'm not surprised."

"It seems Olson got a taste for it. He wasn't linked to other murders at first, but several investigations have since connected him to several other cases. Same MO. He meets a guy in a bar, they get aggressive and get into an argument, then Olson kills them." She spun the mug around. "He likes to use his fists."

Parker sipped his coffee and watched her.

"Then he escalated," she said.

A muscle ticked in Parker's jaw. "How?"

"His next victim was in a bar with his girlfriend. After an altercation, Olson followed them home. It appears he incapacitated the male, and made him watch while he raped the female, then killed them both. Five couples were murdered before he was identified as the perpetrator. He slipped up and left some blood at the last scene. Then he went on the run and ended up in Alaska."

"Hell." Parker frowned, then met her gaze. "I'm not up here because I'm on the run, by the way."

She shot him a faint smile. "Vander vouched for you."

"How do you know Vander?"

"We used Norcross Security to assist on a case in San Francisco once. And I did a seminar with his wife."

Vander's wife, Brynn, was a police detective in San Francisco. Jenna liked the woman a lot.

"How did Olson get free?" Parker asked.

"We're not exactly sure. He was being transported in

a small convoy. Two marshals had him in their vehicle, and they were escorted by two state troopers."

Parker's eyebrows rose. "That's it? You knew what he was capable of and you had four guys on him."

Jenna pulled a face. "It wasn't my decision." She paused. "It looks like he got free of his restraints, over-powered the marshals, and caused a car accident." Anger churned inside her. "The troopers were injured, and he executed the marshals before they could even get out of their vehicle." She clenched her jaw, thinking of Lopez and Calt. "Olson then took their weapons and left on foot."

"So, he's on the run in the wilderness." Parker shook his head. "You'll never find him."

"I will."

"Marshal Sheridan—"

"It's Jenna."

He paused. "You think you know what Ghost Ops involves, but you don't. Olson can fight, track, survive in the wilderness. If he attacks, you won't see or hear him coming. Added to that, he is hugely motivated to not get caught. He won't want to go to prison, and if he's as addicted to killing as you're saying, he won't want to give that up."

She leaned forward. "This is why I need you. You know how he thinks, you have the same training. You can help me find him."

Parker shook his head.

"Please? We both know there's a good chance he'll hurt someone else." She pulled a map out of her pocket, unfolded it, and slapped it on the table. "This is where he escaped his escort." She pointed to a red X on the map. "It's close to Fairbanks, but I don't think he'll head into town."

"He won't."

"I'm guessing he'll try to hide." She met Parker's gaze. "But I know his dark side. Killers like him can't ignore the urge to take a life."

"You know a lot about serial killers?"

Her stomach cramped. More than she'd ever wanted to know. "I do. He won't be able to stop from killing again."

A muscle ticked in Parker's jaw.

"We have a rogue Ghost Ops soldier on the loose. A rogue soldier turned serial killer and rapist. I'm going to stop at *nothing* to bring him in and put him behind bars."

"I believe you."

She reached a hand across the table and touched his. "I need your help."

At the touch, Parker yanked his hand back.

She stilled and watched his face. *What was that about?*

He stared at the map, not meeting her gaze. A groove formed between his eyebrows. "I can't help you. I don't want to get dragged into this."

She watched him rub the scars on his neck, darkness churning in his amber-brown eyes.

Frustration bit at her. She knew Parker Conroy was the key to stopping Kyle Olson. She pulled out a business card and slid it across the table.

"I'm staying at the Frontier Inn, in Fairbanks. If you change your mind, call." She rose.

"I won't."

He sounded sure, but Vander had told her that Parker Conroy was a good man with an unshakable sense of right and wrong. Clearly, he'd been through a lot, and she guessed that there were more scars that she couldn't see.

Maybe he wasn't the man Vander had known anymore.

She hoped that wasn't true.

She'd left the bait, and she hoped that eventually, he'd take it.

Gah, that meant she'd have to wait. And she hated waiting, especially knowing that Olson was out there.

She headed for the front door.

"Wait, you forgot your map," Parker said.

She looked over her shoulder. "Keep it."

That brown gaze bored into her. She wondered what secrets a man like Parker Conroy had. What he kept hidden under that contained exterior of his.

She headed back to her vehicle, praying that he would cave on his decision not to help her.

The clock was ticking.

CHAPTER THREE

Parker paced his small living room. Right then, he wished it was bigger because just a few strides kept bringing him to the wood log wall. He swiveled and paced back.

Night had fallen, and a bird was hooting somewhere outside.

All he could think about was Kyle Olson.

He had a clear image of the guy from their time in Ghost Ops. Olson had reddish-brown hair, a short beard, and an unmemorable face. He just looked like a regular guy.

But he wasn't. He was a killer.

The man was out there. *Somewhere.* A danger to anyone he had contact with.

The man had been an asshole when Parker had known him. Rude, aggressive, violent. Vander had been instrumental in getting him removed from Ghost Ops.

And now he'd turned into a rapist and killer.

Fuck.

Park pressed his hands to the back of his neck and stared out the window at the dense darkness. The marshals wouldn't catch him. He'd been caught once and he wouldn't let it happen again.

The thought of Jenna Sheridan anywhere near Olson froze Park's blood.

She was tough, but Olson wouldn't follow the rules.

Park could find him. Jenna was right about that. He could think like Olson, predict what he'd do next.

Annoyance cut through him. He didn't want to get involved.

When he'd woken up in a hospital bed after he'd escaped his captors, he'd known it was time to get out. Good soldiers had died, Park had failed to save them, and then he'd endured weeks of torture. Weeks of being beaten, cut, and burned. His head was too full of dark shit for him to continue as a soldier.

Maybe if he'd stayed in, he would've turned into a Kyle Olson.

He growled. He wasn't anything like fucking Olson.

On the table, his cellphone vibrated. He glared at it. He got the odd call, but mostly he ignored them.

With a growl, he snatched it up and when he saw Vander's name, his gaze narrowed. He stabbed the screen. "You sicced the US Marshals on me."

There was a beat of silence. "No, just one marshal who needs your help."

Park made a sound. "I'm out. Retired. I just want to be left in peace."

"You're brooding. Stewing in survivor's guilt and what happened to you."

"Yeah, well, when you get tortured for three weeks, I think you earn the right to tell the world to fuck off."

"I'll never give up on you, Park. You're one of mine."

Dammit. There was an iron thread in Vander's voice. He never left any man behind. Even though he'd left Ghost Ops a few years ago, Park knew he'd been pulling strings behind the scenes when Park had been captured. Rattling cages to ensure he was found and rescued.

"I can't do it, Vander."

"Yes, you can. You're one of the strongest men I know, Park. I know what you endured. I know it was a nightmare, but you made it. You survived. And you have the skills to stop Olson. More importantly, you have the instincts. He'll outthink the marshals, but you...he can't escape you."

A muscle ticked in Park's jaw. He could feel himself getting sucked in.

"Jenna is stubborn, dedicated, and dogged," Vander added. "She won't stop until she's found Olson. She needs your help."

"Shit, I am so annoyed at you right now."

"You're one of mine and I'll always have your back. Now, it's time to get out of limbo, Park. Quit dancing around and pick a side. You need me, call." Vander ended the call.

Quit dancing around and pick a side.

Dammit. He grabbed his flannel shirt off the back of his chair and pulled it on over his T-shirt, then he grabbed his keys.

In his head, he mentally called Vander a bunch of

names as he headed for his truck. He slid into his black Dodge Ram and headed for Fairbanks.

When he pulled up in front of the Frontier Inn, he'd decided to try and quit talking himself out of this.

He was going to help Jenna hunt down Kyle Olson.

He pulled into a parking spot and was about to call her, when he saw a young African-American man step out of the bar next door. He was talking on a cellphone, and the way he was dressed—neatly-pressed trousers and a fancy jacket—had Park pegging him as a marshal. Definitely not a Fairbanks local.

Climbing out of the truck, Park headed for the bar. As he neared, he spotted Jenna through the front window. She was sitting at the long, wooden bar, and at a table nearby, were several more men he guessed were law enforcement.

He headed in, then sat on the stool beside her.

When she looked up, relief covered her face. "Drink?"

"Yeah. Beer."

She waved at the bartender. She had the remains of a burger sitting in front of her, along with a glass of red wine. "A beer, please." Then she swiveled toward Parker. "You changed your mind."

"You can't do this alone."

Her chin lifted, a glint in her blue eyes. "I could, but it'll take me longer without you."

His beer arrived. He sat there, silent. Jenna didn't say anything, and he liked that she didn't feel the need to fill the silence.

"I need everything you have on Olson," he said.

"Done."

"Where he's been staying. Friends, acquaintances, places he's frequented. I also need to see the location where he escaped."

She nodded. "Can you track him? We tried a dog, but with no luck."

"I can try. Or I can at least get an idea of where he's headed." Park sipped his beer. He barely tasted it. "He has to be stopped."

"We can both agree on that."

He turned her way and eyed her. "How did you end up a marshal?"

"I always wanted to catch the bad guy. As a kid, I chased the boys in the playground, not to kiss them, but to bend their arm behind their back and arrest them. Sometimes, they cried."

Park smiled. *Shit*. It had been a long time since he'd done that.

"You look surprised you did that," she said. "Not much to smile at lately?"

An itchy feeling made him hunch his shoulders. "Something like that. So, playing marshal in the playground was your inspiration?"

Her smile died away. "No. My father committed a terrible crime and was arrested." She looked back at her drink. "The day he went to prison, I vowed I'd be on the right side of the law and help put people like him away."

Shit. Park knew he'd stepped somewhere very personal for her. He wondered what her father had done.

"Why did you join the military?" she asked.

"My dad was in the Army."

26

"So you followed in his footsteps?"

"I never knew him. He and my mother were killed in a car accident when I was a toddler."

Her expression changed. "I'm sorry."

"Not your fault. I ended up in foster care. No complaints. I had some good homes, and got adopted by a good family when I was twelve. I guess joining the Army was my way of honoring him."

"And then Ghost Ops."

"And then Ghost Ops. Which you know more about than most people."

"I have clearance. I needed intel so I could understand Olson."

"I'm not sure we want to fully understand Olson."

She sipped her wine. "Agreed, but to find him, we need any advantage." She paused. "You miss Ghost Ops?"

"No."

She cocked her head. "Are you going to handle being back in the field?"

He took a long sip of his beer. "Yes."

"I need more than that, Parker. I'm guessing from your...scars, that your military career didn't end the way you hoped."

He locked his gaze on hers. "You aren't shy about asking any questions, are you?"

She shrugged a shoulder. "No. Being shy doesn't help me catch the bad guys."

"No one's just outright asked me about my scars." He paused, a part of him not wanting to share anything. "Why did your father go to prison?"

Something flashed in her eyes. "He murdered inno-cent people."

Shit. That was heavier than he'd guessed. "My Ghost Ops career ended with three weeks of captivity. The Taliban aren't the best hosts."

She sucked in a breath.

"Yeah, it was as bad as you're imagining, but I assure you, I can help you track down Olson."

She watched him for a beat, then nodded. "We have a command post set up in the conference room at the hotel next door. We'll meet in the morning."

"Okay."

"I'll take you to the accident site then, as well. You can meet my team. I have several other marshals here, and we're planning a full-scale search with the help of the state troopers. They're as pissed about this as we are."

Park made a noise.

She frowned. "What?"

"You won't find him."

"We have to try. And now, I have my secret weapon." She tilted her head. "You. You can help me narrow down search locations."

"Did Olson have any friends up here?"

Her frown deepened. "Not that I know of. I'll look into it."

"He needs resources, and then he can disappear. He could steal them, but that would attract attention he doesn't want right now."

"So it's better if he has a friend who gives him what he needs." She toyed with the coaster her drink was resting on. "If he gets away, Parker, and disappears into the wilderness, we'll never find him."

Park set his glass down. "We'll find him."

There was no way in hell that Park would let a killer run free, especially one who'd left a stain on the teams that meant a lot to him. A stain on the memories of the men who'd given their lives fighting for their country.

"You'll be at the hotel in the morning?" Jenna asked.

"I'll be there."

JENNA WAS ALREADY on coffee number two.

She was sitting at her spot at the head of the conference table, surrounded by maps and papers. The other marshals were working in the adjoining conference room. She was waiting for Parker to arrive, and figured he would be here soon.

Owen walked in and set more files down. "Lieutenant Dunford checked in. No sign of Olson."

She figured as much.

Owen crossed his arms. "You sure this Conroy guy can help?"

"Yes."

Her partner sat. "We already have marshals and the state troopers. I don't think we need someone else getting involved."

"We do. Parker Conroy served on the same teams as Olson. He'll be exactly what we need to catch him."

Owen pulled a face. "I know whatever these guys did in the military is classified, and you can't tell me about it, or about this team—" he made air quotes with his fingers "—but it can't be *that* good."

"It is."

Her cellphone rang. When she saw Vic's name on the screen, she rolled her eyes to the ceiling and counted to three. Then, steeling herself, she stabbed at the phone. "Vic."

"You found him yet? I need an update."

"You know this guy's highly trained, so no, we haven't found him yet. We're working on it."

Her ex's ripe curse cut across the line.

Vic was clearly feeling the heat. It was his cost-cutting initiative and arrogant attitude that had caused this.

"You should have assigned more people to the transport detail, Vic."

He made a sound. "I thought you were exaggerating this guy's skills. He's not the only fugitive we're after."

Vic just didn't like to think anyone was better than him.

"You think of screwing me over and making me look bad, Sheridan, then—"

"Vic." Her voice was sharp. "You never actually factor into any of my decisions." Not since she'd dumped him. "I will do my job because I want a criminal like Olson in prison."

Vic was silent. "Sorry, I'm just feeling the pressure. I know you're good at your job, Jenna."

"I am."

He was silent for a moment. "I miss that gung-ho drive of yours."

She resisted the urge to roll her eyes. "I'll call you when I have an update." She ended the call.

"What did you ever see in him?" Owen asked.

"I can't remember." At first, they'd had a camaraderie. She thought they'd worked well together, even if he was often impulsive, and had a habit of hogging the limelight. He was good-looking, he'd showered her with compliments. He'd told her that he liked her strength and intelligence.

Of course, after she'd broken off the relationship, that had soured. Suddenly, she was a ball buster.

No man wants to be emasculated, Jenna. You're not feminine enough. I needed softness. I needed someone who needed me.

She shook her head and thoughts of Vic away.

"Morning."

She glanced up. Parker stood in the doorway.

He looked good. He wore jeans and a black T-shirt that fit his hard chest like a glove. She was well aware of what that chest looked like without the cotton.

Crap, how much had he overheard of her phone call?

"Morning." She stood. "Parker Conroy, this is Deputy Marshal Owen Briggs."

Owen was polite, but she could tell he was still unconvinced. He held out a hand, but Parker just nodded and didn't take it.

"Nice to meet you," Parker said.

She remembered when she'd touched his hand yesterday.

He didn't like to be touched.

Jenna's stomach contracted. Knowing now that he'd

spent three weeks in Taliban captivity, it made sense. *What the hell had they done to him?*

She stood. "Owen, Parker needs to go over everything we have on Olson. Then we'll go and take a look at the accident site."

"We've gone over it already," Owen said. "And the state troopers took the vehicles away. It'll be a waste of time."

"I haven't gone over it." Parker started flipping through a file on the table.

Owen crossed his arms. "I thought you jarheads were allergic to paperwork."

Parker raised a brow. "Look, kid, I'm not here to step on your toes. I'm here to help."

Owen looked like he wanted to argue about the kid comment, but when Jenna shot him a hard look, he just nodded.

"Olson was living in Markell." Parker kept scanning the document.

"Yes. It's a tiny speck of a town, about three hours from here." Owen sat in one of the chairs. "He apparently stuck to himself, but made occasional trips into town. He frequented the bar, and the local store for supplies and ammo."

"Markell is known as a place where people hoping to disappear live," Jenna said. "When law enforcement come to town, many of the residents dissolve into the hills."

Parker flipped a page. "A lot of places in Alaska like that. Olson must have been staying somewhere outside the town." He tapped the page. "But he likes his weapons. The store in town is the only source of ammunition. We need to talk with the store owner." He eyed both of them. "We need to go in quietly, not pull up with sirens and lights and spook people."

Owen straightened. "We know how to blend."

Parker met Jenna's gaze. She bit her lip. She knew Owen didn't blend at all, not with his fondness for designer jackets and tailored pants.

"Okay, let's hit the accident site, then pay—" she checked the file "—Marty Price, proprietor of the Markell Trading Post, a visit."

"It's a three-hour drive," Owen said.

"You don't have to come, kid," Parker said.

Owen straightened. "I'm coming. And I'm not a kid."

Jenna glanced at Parker. "You armed?"

"Yes." There was a faint twitch of his lips. "And yes, I have a permit to carry concealed."

She stood. "Let's go. Every second Olson is out there, he has a better chance of getting away for good."

CHAPTER FOUR

P arker stood on the road, his hands on his hips.

The cars were gone now, but he saw the skid marks on the road and in the dirt beside it.

"The marshals' SUV was here." Jenna motioned. "It was on its roof. The state trooper vehicle was there." She pointed.

Park nodded. "Olson got free of his restraints, then attacked your marshals, and caused the crash. He would have purposely hit the state trooper vehicle." He scanned the surroundings. "He took a marshal's weapon, killed your men, then shot and injured the troopers. Then he took off."

"We know all of this already." Owen stood nearby.

Park ignored the guy. He was young, cocky, and feeling threatened.

Focusing on the ground, Park walked the path that Olson had taken. He imagined climbing out of the car after killing the marshals, and firing at the troopers. Park swiveled. Large, grassy fields flanked the roads, with hills in the distance.

"The scent dog followed a trail through here." Jenna walked in front of him. She was in another pair of jeans today, with a brown jacket. She looked stylish, the denim hugging her ass in a way that was hard to ignore.

Focus on the job, Conroy, not the marshal.

They walked into the field. The grass was knee-high and the ground was muddy.

Owen grumbled. Park saw him glaring at his mud-splattered shoes and felt a spurt of amusement.

"Stay with the SUV if you don't want to get your shoes dirty," Park suggested.

The man's gaze narrowed, and he stubbornly stomped after them.

"The dog lost the scent here." Jenna motioned to a flat patch of grass.

"He knew you'd bring dogs." Park crouched and touched the mud. The pungent scent of rotting leaves and sludge hit him. "He covered himself in mud to disrupt the dog." He looked up and nodded. "He went that way."

Owen frowned. "Mud can throw off the scent?"

"If you know what you're doing." Park rose. "Olson knows what he's doing."

"So, what's that way?" Owen shifted, his shoes squelching in the mud.

"Markell," Park answered.

"Shit," Jenna said.

Owen's eyebrows winged up. "Markell's over a hundred miles from here."

"Olson's fit and has no gear." Park stared into the distance. "He could make that. This terrain won't stop him. Add in the possibility that he hitchhiked part of the way, and he'd have made it back by now."

"He'll connect with acquaintances," Jenna said. "Get supplies and things he needs."

"Yeah." Park nodded. "We need to have that poke around Markell."

Jenna slid her hands into her pockets. "Marty Price won't be happy to see us. It's not the kind of place where people talk to law enforcement. From what the state troopers tell me, everyone's unfriendly, standoffish, and keeps to themselves."

"We'll hit the local bar and look like we belong." Parker looked at Owen at the same time Jenna did.

"What?" the young marshal said.

"I'll drop you back at the hotel," Jenna told him. "You can help the lieutenant coordinate the search once we narrow down Olson's location."

"What? No." Owen shook his head. "I can blend in."

Park raised a brow.

"I *can.*"

"I've got this, Owen," Jenna said. "Parker and I will go in, ask questions, and be back this evening."

"*No.*" Owen straightened. "I'm coming, but I'll stay in the vehicle. You could need backup."

Parker was impressed. The kid had a spine.

Finally, Jenna nodded. "Deal. But you stay out of sight."

"We'll take my truck," Park said. "It'll be less conspicuous than your shiny Tahoe."

They stopped at Parker's cabin and swapped vehicles, then set off.

Several hours later, Parker drove into Markell. It was the afternoon, but the sun wouldn't set until much later, so the day was still bright and sunny.

It didn't help the town much. The sunlight made it look even more rundown and dingy. The main street had a few shops and the bar. Some houses were clustered around the main part of town, and most of the buildings were wood, with faded paint.

He parked in front of the general store.

"Stay here, Owen," Jenna said. "I'm not sure how long we'll be."

In the back seat, the young man huffed out a breath. "I got it. Call me if you need me."

Park eyed the weathered building that housed the Markell Trading Post. He spotted a sign on the front door. "The store's closed for the day."

Jenna raised a brow. "Maybe because Marty Price is out helping a friend?"

"We need to find out where Price lives." Park eyed the rundown bar across the street. A carved sign above the door said it was called Rusty's.

"Keen for a beer?" he asked.

She cocked her head. "It just so happens I am. Wait a sec." She pulled off her jacket, then unbuttoned her shirt. Park's eyes widened.

But when she slipped the shirt off, she was wearing a black tank top underneath. She opened the passenger door of the Ram and tossed the jacket and shirt on the seat. Her gun followed, then she unclipped the badge from her belt.

She reached inside her pocket and pulled out a small tube of lipstick. She looked in the side mirror as she painted the bold red on her lips. Then she fluffed her hair in the reflection of the car window. Finally, she tugged the neckline of her tank down—showing off a healthy dose of cleavage.

She spun and smiled. Her entire demeanor changed. She looked looser, a little wilder.

This should be interesting.

"Come on, babe. Buy me a beer." She slipped her arm through his.

His muscles tensed at her touch.

She stilled. "Sorry, is this okay?" She started to pull away. "I get that you don't like being touched."

He gripped her arm, keeping it twined with his. "It's okay."

She eyed his face. "You're sure?"

"Yes."

She nodded. "All right, then."

As they headed toward the bar, Park realized something.

A part of him didn't mind the lovely marshal pressed against his side.

THE BAR WAS WELL beyond seedy.

As she stepped inside, the wooden floor creaked, and

was sticky with... Jenna didn't know what and didn't want to know.

A few rough-looking types were dotted around, sitting in the booths and at the bar. Two guys with huge, bushy beards were playing pool at a rickety, worn pool table. They stopped to watch her and Parker walk in.

She flashed them a saucy smile.

"Baby, I need a drink. I'm *so* thirsty after all that driving."

Parker slid a hand down and around her hip. She barely controlled her jolt.

"I'll get you whatever you want, sweetheart."

She liked his hand on her a little too much. Clearing her throat, she slid onto a stool at the bar. The bartender was a man in his fifties, with a weathered face, tattoos around his neck, and shaved gray hair.

"What can I get ya?"

"Two Jack Daniel's, please. No ice."

He gave her a chin lift.

Parker leaned against the bar and casually scanned the room. He'd no doubt clocked everyone sitting inside. Then he leaned into her, his mouth close to her ear. "No sign of Price or Olson."

Jenna hadn't expected Olson to be sitting in the bar. Still, a girl could hope.

The bartender plonked the glasses down in front of her. She grabbed hers and handed the other one to Parker. She clinked her glass against his and tossed it back.

It burned. It had been a long while since she'd had

whiskey. She wasn't much of a drinker, but she did like a glass of red wine on occasion.

Parker looked amused and sipped at his drink

"That hit the spot." She whirled. "Beer next, please." She perused the lineup. "I'll have an Alaskan Amber."

The bartender's lips twitched. "A girl who likes her drink."

Jenna winked. "A girl who likes to have some fun."

A moment later, he set the beer down in front of her. "You folks just passing through?"

"Something like that. I'm Jen, and this is my man, Con."

Parker lifted his drink.

"We're on a little Alaskan vacation." Jenna sipped her beer. "If we find the right place, we might stay awhile."

"Not much around here," the bartender said.

"That's what I like about it..." Jenna smiled and touched her tongue to her upper lip. "What's your name?"

"Rusty."

"This is your place?"

"Sure is." The bar owner's chest puffed up. "Rusty's is always open."

Park sipped his drink. "Unlike the local store. We saw it was closed."

"That's rare," Rusty said. "The owner, Marty, took a day off."

"I saw there's an apartment above the shop," Jenna said. "Must be hard to take time off when you live where you work."

"Nah, Marty rents the apartment out. He's got a cabin out on Bay Mountain Road."

Bingo.

"Any cabins for rent around here?" Jenna asked.

"Maybe." Rusty shrugged a shoulder. "Marty would know."

Jenna flashed a smile. "Thanks, Rusty."

She turned and leaned into Parker. "How about a game of pool, baby?"

He set his glass down. "Sounds good."

The old-timers had finished their game, and the pool table was empty.

She racked the balls while Parker chalked his cue. She quickly pulled her phone out and texted the info on Marty to Owen.

Then she pulled Parker in close. His hands clamped on her hips, like he wasn't sure if he wanted to pull her closer or push her away.

"Is this okay?" she whispered. "If it makes you uncomfortable..."

"It's fine." His voice sounded like gravel, but he pulled in a breath, tucking some of her hair behind her ear. His fingers brushed her skin, leaving warm tingles behind.

Keeping in character, she nuzzled into his chest. "I've got Owen narrowing down where Marty Price's cabin is."

"It's scary how good you are at this."

She tipped her head back and smiled. "You haven't seen anything yet, baby." She studied his face. She slid her hands up his arms and registered how taut his muscles were. "You're sure that you're okay?"

"I...haven't been this close to anyone since..." A muscle ticked beside his eye. "A long time."

She started to pull away, but his hands tightened, holding her where she was.

"I don't want to hurt you."

"I'm okay," he repeated.

What the hell had they done to him? "You have nothing to prove to me."

He shook his head, then released her. "You can break, sweetheart."

They played a game of pool. Their bodies brushed a few times, and Jenna found her body warming, reacting to his. She kept glancing at his face to gauge his reaction. His face was blank, making it impossible to read.

She shook her head. She was in the middle of a manhunt and didn't have time to drool over a man.

She took the next shot, leaning over. Sensing his attention, she glanced back and caught him looking at her ass.

Her lips curved. "Con, are you focused?"

"I am." His dark gaze flicked up. "Just not on the game."

There was a thump of heavy footsteps on the wood. A mammoth man in red flannel stepped up to the table. He had a bushy, red beard and a hard face.

"I'm playing with her next," he rumbled.

Parker calmly chalked the end of his cue. "Not happening."

The mountain man was several inches taller and broader than Parker. Jenna clutched her cue, ready to react if needed.

"I do what I want," the man announced.

"I don't care. She's my woman, and she's not playing with you."

The man took a threatening step forward. "Who's going to stop me? You?"

"Actually, she's perfectly capable of stopping you herself, but look, just go back to your buddies." Parker's voice dropped to a lethal level. "So you don't get hurt."

That tone gave her shivers.

The mountain man was not so bright. He puffed up his chest. "I'm not afraid of you."

Parker lowered his arms. "You should be."

With a growl, the man swung a fist and bellowed.

Parker calmly sidestepped, then cracked the cue over the man's back. The wood broke in half. The mountain man stumbled forward, then Parker punched him and slammed him into the pool table.

The man slid off the table and crashed to the floor, out cold. The man's friends stood, and when Parker swiveled their way and shot them a look, they slowly sat back down.

"Sweetheart, it's time to go," Parker said. "I think we're done here."

She watched him and licked her lips. Watching him take down that guy had been...hot. "Okay, baby."

He slid an arm around her, and she twined her arms around his neck. He tensed, then relaxed. She slapped a kiss to his cheek.

Their gazes locked and she felt a shot of pure heat in her belly. That intensity of his radiated off him, like a caress on her skin. He felt like a contained storm.

"Sorry," she whispered. "I shouldn't have—"

He hauled her closer, then his mouth was on hers.

She opened her lips, and his tongue boldly slipped inside. He cupped the back of her head, and she melted against him. The warmth of him hit her, the taste of him. Desire was a bright burn inside her and she moaned into his mouth.

"Get a room," someone cried. It was followed by a lot of hooting and hollering.

Jenna stepped back and blinked. She felt dazed.

Parker had that inscrutable look on his face again, but she got the impression he was a little knocked off balance.

She swallowed and managed a shaky smile. She raised her voice. "We might just do that. Bye, fellas."

As she walked out of the bar, she was a little unsteady and her panties a little damp.

"We need to go," she said, not meeting his gaze.

When was the last time any kiss had affected her like this? When had she ever let a man close enough to rattle her with just one touch?

She already knew the answer to that question. *Never.*

CHAPTER FIVE

"Turn here," Owen said from the back seat.

Park turned onto a long, winding driveway. It wasn't well-kept. There were potholes and clumps of long grass.

He drove on, maneuvering around the worst of the potholes. The entire time, he was fighting his awareness of Jenna sitting in the seat beside him. Her lush, floral perfume was buried in his senses.

He'd kissed her.

And she'd kissed him back.

Then, they'd kissed the hell out of each other.

His hands tightened on the steering wheel. For the first time in a really long time, he'd wanted someone to touch him. He'd wanted her hands on his body.

They hit a deep pothole and the truck shuddered. *Shit.* He steered them free.

"Okay?" She shot him a look.

"Fine." *Focus on the damn mission, Conroy.*

But it was harder than it should be. He'd never had a

problem focusing on a mission before. He'd been known for his laser-focused intensity.

Then again, he'd never gone on a mission with someone like Jenna.

He liked her touch. He should be glad that he wasn't as screwed up as he'd thought. But another part of him was shouting at him.

That part of him didn't want to feel, didn't want to get close to anyone.

His hands flexed on the steering wheel again. Jenna wouldn't be here long. He'd help her find Olson and then his life would go back to peace and quiet.

A stand of trees came into view. There was a cabin nestled in the center.

"Nice," Jenna said.

Her sarcasm was clear. The wooden cabin looked pretty rough. It appeared Marty Price had added on to it at some stage, and the new additions didn't match the original cabin. It made the entire structure look lopsided. An old, wooden shed sat just beyond the cabin.

"No sign of a car," Park murmured.

"Maybe he loaned it to Olson," Owen suggested.

Park stopped the truck. They all got out, studying their surroundings. As they headed toward the cabin, Park thought it was quiet. Too quiet for his liking.

Jenna strode ahead—sure and steady. He was realizing how driven she was. Determined to take Olson down. To help people.

He picked up speed, scanning ahead.

Jenna knocked on the weathered front door. "Mr. Price?"

Park glanced in one window. This cabin made his place look like a palace. It looked like Price wasn't big on cleaning. "There's ammo on the table." Along with dirty plates. "Looks like there are two plates on the table."

"Maybe Price had company?" Jenna's gaze sharpened. She tried the handle and it turned. She cautiously opened the door.

She pulled out her handgun and nodded at Owen. The other marshal did the same.

"Go left," she said.

Park waited in the doorway as the marshals split, and cleared the small cabin in just under a minute.

"Clear," Owen said, coming out of the bedroom.

Jenna opened and closed a small closet. "Clear." She pulled a face, sliding her gun back into its holster. "He's not here."

There was no sign of Marty Price. Park checked the papers resting on the table. One was a map. There was nothing marked on it, but it was folded to display an area a few hundred miles south from there, centered on Drifter Lake.

He knew of the area. He'd looked into it when he was looking to buy his cabin. It was remote, but there was a lodge that was open in the summer, and a few cabins in the area.

"Let's check out back," Jenna said.

They headed back out the front door and circled the cabin. The grass was overgrown, but a path had been beaten down toward the shed. The structure was made of weathered, wooden planks that had, at one point in history, been painted red. One side of it was open to the elements, and an old truck was parked under it.

The place looked like a decent wind would blow it down.

Owen moved ahead of Park, and he kept one eye on the junior marshal, becoming more impressed with each passing moment. The kid had decent skills, and was alert and observant.

They walked along the shed and Park spotted footprints in the dirt. He slowed down, then crouched. Two pairs of boots, by the look of it. One had a distinctive looking tread.

"Let's search the shed." Owen reached out to pull the lopsided wooden door open.

Park heard a sound, one his brain registered in a millisecond.

A shotgun getting pumped.

Park spun and slammed into Owen.

The marshal stiffened. "What the—?"

He knocked the young guy to the ground, just as a shotgun blast ripped through the wood of the shed.

More blasts reverberated, and wood splinters rained over them.

"Stay down," Park growled.

He lifted his head and saw Jenna running, gun in hand. She was headed for the open end of the shed.

Fuck this.

Park moved into a crouch. He waited. There was another shotgun blast, and he felt a chip of wood clip his neck.

After a pause, he knew Price was reloading, and Park launched himself through the ruined wood panels.

He crashed into the shadowed shed, he saw the older man instantly. Price stood with his feet spread, shotgun in hand.

Park charged him. He kicked the man, then wrenched the gun away. Price reached for his belt and pulled out a long, hunting knife.

"That's a bad idea," Park said.

"This is my place. You're trespassing!" The old man's thin, gray hair fell in straggly strands around his weathered face. "Man's got a right to defend himself."

"We're US marshals, and you know why we're here."

Marty Price lifted the knife and moved to the left. "We don't like pigs or feds around here."

Park shook his head. "Just put it down. I don't want to hurt you."

The old man snorted. "You can try, boy." He darted forward, slicing out with the knife.

The man was faster than Park had given him credit for. Park dodged, and chopped a hand to Price's back. The man grunted.

"Last chance, old man."

"Fuck you!" He swung fast.

Park didn't really want to hurt the guy. He whirled, and felt a lick of heat on his side. He ignored it, then rammed a blow to the man's arm. Price cried out and dropped the knife on the dusty floor.

Park yanked the man's arms behind his back, and kicked his legs out from under him.

Just as he dropped to his knees, Jenna appeared. She had her Glock aimed at Price's head.

"You okay?" she asked Parker.

"Fine."

She put her weapon away, then pulled her handcuffs off her belt.

"Martin Price, you're under arrest for attacking US Marshals. We're taking you into custody."

The man got a mulish, sullen look on his face.

Owen stepped inside. "Everyone okay?" He had a cut under one eye and looked a little pale.

"Yes, everyone's all right," Jenna said. "What about you?"

"I'm alive." The younger man cleared his throat and looked at Park. "Um, thanks."

Park gave the man a chin lift.

Jenna stepped in front of Price. "Where is Kyle Olson?"

Price sniffed. "Who?"

"Don't play games with me. The man is dangerous. We know that you're friends with him. Did you help him escape?"

Price sniffed again.

Jenna grabbed the man's gray hair and yanked it back. He hissed out a breath.

"He's a killer. Is that the kind of man you are, one who protects a killer?"

"He said you made it all up," Price yelled. "The cops framed him and are out to get him."

"It's not made up," Park said.

Price glanced at him. "You've got the same look as Olson."

"Except I don't kill for fun."

"Or rape," Jenna added.

Price jerked. "Rape?"

"Oh, did your buddy forget to mention that bit?" Jenna said. "How he ties men up, makes them watch while he rapes their girlfriend or partner."

Price's throat bobbed as he swallowed. "I don't approve of hurting women."

"Then tell me where he is."

"You won't find him. He's long gone."

"You gave him supplies?" she asked.

The man nodded. "Food, camping gear, and clothes." He paused. "Weapons and ammo."

"Dammit," she muttered.

"He left on foot?" Park asked.

Price nodded again. "The one thing he wanted more than anything was the damn boots he'd ordered."

"Boots?" Jenna prodded.

"A pair of Anvil tactical hiking boots. Olson swears by 'em. Had to special order them for him."

"Where is he going?" Jenna demanded.

"I don't know."

"If I find out—"

"I don't know! He wouldn't tell me."

"There's a map inside," Park said. "It shows an area around Drifter Lake, south of here."

Jenna's mouth flattened. "What do you know about it?"

"It's remote, but there are some people who live

there, a lodge. and a public camping ground. It would be easy for him to get his supplies."

"He's been there before," Price said suddenly. "Hunting. He mentioned it once."

Jenna straightened. "Owen, call the state troopers. Mr. Price here needs processing. He shot at US Marshals."

Price's shoulders sagged.

"What's the plan?" Park asked.

"The plan is that we map out a search of the Drifter Lake area and find our guy."

Park nodded. Preferably before Olson hurts anyone else.

JENNA WAS FIGHTING off tiredness when Parker pulled into the parking lot in front of her hotel.

The state troopers had taken Marty Price into custody, and Owen had gone with them. She and Parker had pulled Price's place apart. The map was the only useful clue they'd found.

"You really think Olson has gone to the Drifter Lake area?" she asked.

"Yeah, I do." Parker pulled to a stop and cut the engine.

"Thanks for your help today. And for saving Owen." It had been Parker's quick actions that had saved her marshal's life.

"He's cocky, but he has good instincts. I wasn't going to let him get shot."

"He's learning." She eyed him. "Let me buy you dinner? There's a decent Chinese takeout down the road. We can eat while we scour the map and plan our search for Olson."

Parker was quiet a second, then he nodded. "I like Chinese. Used to miss it when I was deployed."

Soon, they were sitting in the conference room eating fried rice and Kung Pao chicken out of takeout boxes.

"It looks like the Drifter Lake Lodge gets a fair number of tourists in the summer," Jenna said. "Surely Olson wouldn't risk going there."

Parker ate a forkful of food. "Agreed, but there are cabins close by." A groove formed on his brow. "And possible victims, if he gets the urge to kill again."

She hoped he didn't. "I will find him before that happens." She had to.

Memories of her father hit her. Mostly, she tried not to think about the man, but old memories liked to blindside her, especially when she was tired.

There were the images of the kind, loving man who'd thrown her in the air, read to her, and taken her on endless trips to the zoo.

But they were overlaid with the crime scene photos of his victims. The poor women he'd mutilated and killed.

Parker leaned back in his chair. "This job's in your blood."

More than he knew. "It is. I love it. I love knowing that I'm helping and making the world a little safer." Making up for the terror her father had caused. "And I'm good at it."

"I can tell."

"You were good at Ghost Ops. Vander told me that you were one of the best." And she'd seen some of his skills up close and personal. Watching him read the accident site and save Owen at Marty Price's place. It went beyond training. He had instincts most people didn't.

"I felt the same about it as you do about your job," he said. "But sometimes you get used up, burned out." He set his fork down.

"I'm sorry, Parker, about what you went through."

He was quiet for a beat. "My friends call me Park."

Her lips quirked. "Park."

"I came back alive. On the mission when I got captured, good men and women lost their lives. Young people who had their whole lives ahead of them."

Her heart squeezed. "I'm sorry."

He nodded. "I know you lost men this week."

"Yes. I understand. It isn't just the grief, but the feeling that you failed them. If I'd just been faster, or done something different, that I could have saved them..."

A flash of dark emotion crossed his face and was quickly gone. "Yeah."

She cleared her throat. "Your scars...they don't hurt anymore?"

"No." He touched his neck. "It took the docs a while to put me back together, but I was one of the lucky ones."

She knew his torture had changed him. Knew that it haunted him. It was why he'd come to Alaska.

They finished eating, then Parker rose, stacking their empty boxes. She spotted a dark patch on his black T-shirt.

"Is that blood on your shirt?"

He looked down. "It's nothing."

She popped to her feet and circled the table. "You're bleeding. That's *not* nothing, Park." She pulled the hem of his shirt up. "Let me see." Then her eyebrows winged up. "You did this?"

"It stopped the bleeding."

She stared at the wad of tissues held in place with some duct tape.

"Jesus." She pulled the makeshift bandage off and ignored his wince. There was an ugly cut underneath. "This needs proper treatment, Park. Not whatever this half-assed mess is."

His expression turned stubborn. "I'm not going to the hospital."

She rolled her eyes. "Stay. I have a first aid kit in the SUV."

She hustled outside, and grabbed the first aid kit from the Tahoe. He was still sitting with his ass against the table when she returned.

"Shirt off," she ordered.

"Yes, ma'am." He pulled his shirt over his head.

She'd thought about that muscled chest and abs a few times over the last day. His hard muscles tempted a woman to touch. She pulled open the first aid kit and got out some wipes and started cleaning the blood off his skin.

He hissed.

She glanced up. "Does that hurt?"

"No."

Stubborn man. "It's not too deep."

"Price got lucky. Nicked me."

"You should've told me."

"It was fine."

She realized they were standing close together. She felt the heat pumping off him and smelled the scent of his skin. It wasn't cologne, just soap or shower gel. Park didn't strike her as a man who wore fancy cologne.

"I'm going to put a bit of glue in it."

He grunted. She figured it wasn't the first time he'd been glued back together. Her gaze moved over his scars. She saw a circular scar that had to be a bullet wound, along with the healed cuts and burn marks.

Sympathy moved through her. His torture must have been agony. Three weeks of pain, not knowing if anyone was coming for him. Her chest was so tight it was hard to breathe. She knew he'd hate any pity.

She focused on treating his new wound. When she was done, she placed a bandage over the cut. Her fingers brushed his skin.

She heard him draw in a sharp breath and looked up. He was watching her with his dark gaze.

She let her hands drop to her sides. "Sorry."

A muscle ticked in his jaw. "It's fine. Like I said, haven't liked anyone close to me for a long time."

A part of her brain screamed at her to step back, but she couldn't move. She couldn't look away. Electricity seemed to fill the air. It was just the two of them. Alone.

She remembered the kiss in the bar and flutters filled her stomach. She wasn't used to flutters. She liked control. "In the bar, when we kissed..."

"I liked that." His voice was low and gritty.

She sucked in a breath.

"I liked you touching me, Jenna."

She swallowed. "Look, I have to stay focused on my job, on hunting down Olson."

"It's always a job with you?"

She lifted her chin. "Yes."

"I have no plans to stop you from doing your job." He slid his hand around the back of her neck. "You smell too damn good."

She closed her eyes, trying to fight it.

His head lowered, his mouth hovering over hers. "I don't want this either."

"You trying to convince me or yourself?"

He groaned, then he pressed his mouth to hers.

She didn't pull away. No, completely ruled by instinct, she leaned into him and kissed him back. The taste of him was intoxicating. His lips moved over hers, the kiss hot and deep and oh-so-good. With just the touch of his lips and tongue, he owned her. There was no escape. She didn't lie to herself. She didn't want to escape.

His tongue tangled with hers and hot desire ignited in her belly. She wanted so much more than a kiss. Not once had she felt like this with Vic.

The reminder of that debacle crashed through her.

Jenna stumbled back, gripping the waistband of his jeans to stay upright. "This isn't happening." She hated that her legs felt weak.

"Agreed," he bit out. "Neither of us want this." His intense gaze was locked on her, his chest rising and falling.

Then she went up on her toes and pressed another

kiss to his mouth. Her hands pressed to his side, and she felt muscles and scars under her fingers.

They broke apart again, both of them panting, and short of breath.

"Catching Olson has to be my number one priority," she said.

He nodded. "And I haven't got anything that's good for you. For anyone. I'd better head home."

He pulled away and walked past her. And against their control, their hands shifted, their fingers brushing.

She saw his chest hitch. "Goodnight, Marshal Sheridan."

"Goodnight, Park."

Jenna stood there, alone, trying to process what had happened. She closed her eyes. She was pretty sure she was in trouble and it had nothing to do with the dangerous fugitive she was hunting.

CHAPTER SIX

He'd slept well, but just not long enough. Park stepped into the shower and dipped his head under the spray.

He'd already packed his duffel bag for heading to Drifter Lake with Jenna.

Jenna.

He could still taste her, still feel her. She'd been in his dreams all night.

He groaned. He didn't want an attraction like this. He didn't want to feel so damn much. He didn't want a woman, especially not one who understood him, who saw right through him.

Park didn't want anyone seeing his demons.

All his Ghost Ops buddies had fallen in love and married. Hell, even grumpy Shep had taken the fall. Park didn't need it, didn't want it. He just wanted to be left alone.

In his head, he pictured Jenna in the bar. That beaming smile, her cleavage and toned arms on display.

But it wasn't just her looks. She was smart as hell, tough, tenacious.

He slid his hand down his body and circled his cock. Just thinking about her made him hard.

"*Fuck.*" His voice echoed off the tiles. He stroked and imagined that kiss in the conference room. Jenna ran hot. She had passion under all the rules and competence.

She wouldn't be a quiet, passive lover. No, she'd give as good as she got.

He stroked faster. He imagined her there, her hands on him, her mouth on him. He imagined her dropping to her knees in front of him...

He came. *Hard.*

Park groaned through the rush of pleasure, his release splattering on the tiles before it was quickly washed away. He slapped a hand to the wall and sucked in air.

The last waves of pleasure rippled through him.

"*Shit.*" He wasn't supposed to be jerking off thinking about her.

He flicked the water to cold and made himself stay under the spray. Finally, he turned the water off, got out, and dried off. He forced his brain to move on autopilot and not think about anything. He changed the bandage on his cut. Jenna had done a good job on it. *Jenna.*

Locking down his thoughts, he ate some toast and drank some coffee standing up in his kitchen, then he left a plate out for Red. He stood out on the deck, searching the trees. There was no sign of the squirrel.

"I might be gone for a few days."

Hell, he was talking to a squirrel. With a shake of his head, he went back inside and locked up the cabin. Then he was climbing into his truck. He turned the radio on and aimed for Fairbanks.

When he pulled into the Frontier Inn, he was ready. Focused.

He wanted Olson behind bars. Then, Jenna Sheridan would go home. Park's hand flexed. Lifting his chin, he walked into the hotel.

Unsurprisingly, Jenna was already at the conference table, poring over some files.

"Morning," he said.

She looked up and sent him a distracted smile. "Hey. I hope you slept well and are ready for a big day."

He gave her a chin lift. "Yeah."

She tapped the map on the table. "We have the search quadrants planned out around the Drifter Lake area. We'll head out in pairs and check in regularly." She paused. "You're with me, and we're heading to the Drifter Lake Lodge, posing as guests."

Park nodded. *Great, he'd be alone with Jenna.*

"Good morning." Owen hustled in, holding three takeout coffee cups. "I finally found a place that makes a decent mocha."

He set a cup in front of Jenna. "Cappuccino, extra shot."

"I knew there was a reason I kept you around."

Owen turned. "Um..." He held up a cup. "I got you a cappuccino, too."

It looked like the kid had softened toward him. "Thanks." Park took the coffee.

"It's a pretty weak thank you for saving my life."

Park sipped, then held the cup up. "I've had worse thank yous."

Owen nodded.

"And you're welcome," Park added.

They all sat at the table.

"Owen is heading out with some of the other marshals and state troopers. They're forming search teams to search here, here, and here." Jenna tapped areas surrounding Drifter Lake. "Whatever it takes, we're going to find Olson. We need to flush him out." Her mouth flattened. "He's killed two good men, and I won't let that stand."

Owen nodded. "Let's do this."

Jenna glanced at Park. "You look serious."

"Olson won't make it easy."

"I know, but we're up for the challenge. We *can't* let him get away." She glanced at Owen. "You warn the state troopers not to take any chances. I don't want anyone else hurt."

Owen nodded.

Then she rose. "I'm going to get my gear." She stalked out of the conference room.

Park watched her stride away, filled with purpose. She was so damn dedicated. His hand curled into a fist.

Olson wouldn't go down without a fight. Park would do everything he could to keep Jenna safe.

He wondered just how much this hunt would take out of them all.

JENNA PACKED the gear in the back of the Tahoe. She had a personal bag, some camping gear, and general supplies.

"Ready?"

Park's deep voice made her turn. Was she ready to be alone with a man who got to her in so many ways?

She'd spent years forging her career in a man's world. Years doing her bit to make up for the evil her father had perpetrated. She'd vowed never to let anything, let alone a man, derail her. Vic had been a close call and a lesson. Still, it hadn't taken her long to realize he'd hurt her pride and not her heart. She'd never been at risk of falling in love.

Yet, looking at Parker Conroy made her feel things.

She pulled in a deep breath. "I'm ready."

He grabbed her arm. "Don't worry. We'll find him."

She nodded. "I'm just worried who he'll hurt before we do."

"Hopefully, he stays well clear of people until we run him down." Park paused. "You driving?"

She nodded.

Without a reply, he got into the passenger seat. Well, a man who wasn't going to fight her to drive. Parker was a rare breed.

Soon, they were on the road. She fiddled with the radio. "I suppose you like country or rock."

"I don't care. I have what you'd call an eclectic taste."

She settled for a mixed-variety station. "Oh, so you don't mind some Taylor Swift?"

His lips twitched. "No, I don't. And I love some Rhianna."

With a smile, she focused on driving.

The scenery was so different to Virginia. She'd lived there several years, close to the US Marshals Headquarters, though she was on the road a lot. Right now, there was green as far as she could see, with magnificent mountains rising up in the distance. Fields of colorful wildflowers added splashes of brilliant hues.

"I see why you chose to move here. It's beautiful."

He was silent for a moment. "I came here to be as far away from people as I could."

Her heart thumped. Because he'd been locked in a cell and subjected to who knew what. She hurt for him. "I'm sorry."

He glanced her way. "For what?"

"For those demons that are making you run."

His mouth flattened. "I'm not running."

"Okay."

"I'm *not*." He huffed out a breath. "I've seen the worst people can do. I've earned the right not to deal with them anymore."

"I would've thought you'd seen some of the best people can do too, Park."

"I have. Some of those men and women—true, honest-to-God heroes—got blown to pieces because I wasn't fast enough to save them. When I think of them..." He shook his head and looked out the side window.

Her heart squeezed. She heard the guilt tangled up with so many emotions. He was strong, tough, yet he'd seen and done things that had worn him down. He'd been tortured. He'd survived when others hadn't. All that had left him scarred—inside and out.

"Your ex sounds like a douchebag," Park said.

She accepted the change of subject. "He is. Of epic proportions."

Park looked back at her. "What happened?"

"We had a few decent dates, then he cheated. With a twenty-something-year-old college girl. They're married now."

"The guy must be an idiot."

She raised a brow.

"To risk something with a smart, attractive, competent woman like you for a taste of anything else."

She felt a flush of heat. "I consider it a lucky escape. I don't give him, or his young wife, much thought at all."

"But he left his mark."

Yeah, her experience with Vic had rattled her confidence. She hated that Park saw that. When she'd discovered her smiling, loving father was a killer, her life had imploded. She'd vowed to never let a man fool her like that. Vic had come too damn close.

"Life leaves its mark, Park. For better and worse. We learn and grow, and we can't let it break us."

She felt his gaze on her but she didn't look his way.

Up ahead, she glimpsed something in the distance. She leaned forward, and soon she made out an old truck pulled over on the side of the road. Its hood was up, steam rising from it.

"What's this?" They hadn't seen anyone for miles.

Park peered forward. "Looks like someone needs help."

Jenna flicked on the indicator and pulled over behind them.

Two guys straightened. One waved a hand at them and shot them a friendly smile. They were both late thirties, wearing jeans and flannels. One had short, brown hair, while the other had long, messy blond hair.

She watched them a second longer, her gaze narrowing.

"I don't think they need help," Parker said dryly.

No, she'd picked up the vibe, too.

This was a trap.

"Guess it's their unlucky day," she said.

Park gave her a half smile. "This might be fun." He pushed open his door.

They approached the truck. She didn't see any sign of weapons, but it didn't mean the men didn't have any.

"You guys have car trouble?" Jenna asked.

"Yeah." The one with long hair approached her, a wide, friendly smile pasted on his face.

One that didn't reach his eyes.

"What's the problem?" Parker asked.

He was on the other side of the vehicle, and somehow, he'd dialed back that intensity of his. His shoulders were hunched, his eyes low, and he wasn't setting off their radars.

"Actually, nothing's wrong." Short Hair whipped a gun up and aimed it at Park. "Give us your keys, wallet, and cellphones."

Long Hair grinned. "And I want a few minutes alone with Blondie here."

"You sure about that?" Jenna asked.

The man frowned at her. She clearly wasn't reacting

the way he expected. She met Park's gaze. He gave her a small nod.

Then, he exploded into action. He kicked the gun from Short Hair's hand, then landed a hard punch to the man's face.

Long Hair lunged and made a grab for Jenna. She bent her legs, gripped his arm, and yanked.

He made a surprised sound and stumbled forward. She rammed her knee up between his legs.

Now, he made a gurgle.

"Get down, you idiot." She kicked his legs out from under him and pressed a hand to his shoulder. He dropped to his knees in the dirt.

Across the truck, she watched Park slam his guy face first into the hood.

That's when she saw a flash of movement *under* the vehicle.

"Park, watch out! There's a third guy under the truck." She kneed her guy in the face, and watched as he toppled to the ground, out cold. She rushed to circle around the vehicle.

As she got there, Park shoved Short Hair at her. She grabbed the man, and rammed him against the hood again.

Tattooed arms snaked out from under the truck, trying to grab Park's ankles.

He dodged, then grabbed the guy and dragged him out.

The man cursed and twisted, but Park pinned him to the ground with one boot in the center of his back. Leaning down, he yanked the man's arms together.

"Park." She tossed him a set of handcuffs.

He caught them, then cuffed the man.

"Gentlemen," Jenna said. "You're under arrest by the authority of the US Marshals."

Short Hair lifted his head and looked back over his shoulder. "*Fuck.*"

She met Park's gold-brown gaze, and he smiled at her. The first real one she'd seen.

They made a good team.

CHAPTER SEVEN

B y the time the state troopers had come and arrested their would-be thieves, it was late when Jenna and Parker reached the Drifter Lake Lodge.

Lieutenant Dunford had called Jenna and asked her to quit finding trouble. The three assholes they'd arrested apparently had rap sheets, and had been preying on tourists on remote roads for several weeks. They wouldn't be attacking anyone else for a long time.

Park pulled to a stop in front of the lodge. The main lodge was a low, wooden building, with large, potted plants flanking the front entry. In the growing darkness, he catalogued a number of cute, redwood cabins dotted among the trees by the lake.

"This is nice." Jenna grabbed her bag out of the back of the Tahoe.

Park took it from her and lifted his own bag, as well.

"I can carry my bag, Conroy."

"I know." He turned and headed up the steps.

He was pretty sure there was nothing that Jenna

Sheridan couldn't do. She was the most competent, self-sufficient woman he'd met.

The way she'd handled the guys today... It had turned him on. They'd worked together like they'd been doing it for years. The only people he'd shared something like that with were his Ghost Ops teammates.

He stepped inside and the piney scent of a candle hit him. The place looked warm and welcoming, with lots of wood and a vase of wildflowers on the front desk.

"You must be our newlyweds, Mr. and Mrs. Parker." An older woman hurried forward. She was round with a happy smile, her brown hair curling around her face.

Newlyweds? Park hid his jolt.

"That's right." Jenna grabbed his hand. "I'm Jen, and this is Con."

"Welcome to the Drifter Lake Lodge. Now, you're in luck. We've upgraded you to our honeymoon cabin." The woman clapped her hands together. "It's right on the lake and *very* romantic."

"Oh, that's wonderful," Jenna said.

Shit. It sounded like torture to him.

"Come and let's get the registration complete." The woman moved behind the wooden counter. "Oh, I almost forgot, I'm Velma."

"It's beautiful here, Velma." Jenna smiled. "I'm sorry we're a bit late. We had car trouble."

Velma's homey face creased. "Oh, no. My Ross can help you. He's good with engines."

"Oh, we got it sorted. But thank you."

"Ross is a jack of all trades." Pride oozed from her.

"Out here, we have to be able to do a little bit of everything."

"Do you have many other guests right now?" Jenna asked.

Jenna was good. She sounded friendly and casual, and Velma was completely unaware that she was being interrogated.

"Not many. More are arriving in a few weeks as the weather warms up. We have a lovely young couple from Canada who are celebrating their first wedding anniversary. We have a man from Australia. Handsome fellow. He's a bit of an adventurer who's traveling around the world. And an older couple from Norway." Velma whipped out a map. "Are you planning some fishing or hiking?"

"Absolutely," Jenna said. "Con and I love to hike."

"We have a few marked trails around the lake, otherwise it's all on you to hike where you want. This map has our trails." She set it on the counter. "Most people stick close to the lake. You'll need to keep an eye out for bears and other wildlife. Do you have bear spray?"

"We do," Park said.

"Excellent. The scenery here is so beautiful. Once Ross and I saw it, we fell in love and never left. I'm sure you'll love it too."

"Do many other people live close by?" Park asked.

"Not too close. There are a few people with cabins in the area. Don't worry, they keep to themselves, so you'll have your privacy." Velma winked. "I know how important that is to newlyweds."

Jenna studied the map. "What's this?" She pointed at a spot.

"Oh, that's an old hunting cabin. Hunters use it occasionally, otherwise it's empty. It's very basic and a little far out for our guests. The trail gets a bit tricky leading up to it."

Jenna nodded, but shot Park a glance.

It was a good place for Olson to hide.

"Your husband is a man of few words," Velma said to Jenna. "Just like my Ross." She circled the counter again, holding an old-fashioned key with a large wooden tag attached to it. "Come, I'll point out your cabin. Oh, we have Wi-Fi, and decent cell reception here at the lodge, but once you head out, it gets spotty. Breakfast and dinner are served here in the lodge, in our dining room. I do love to cook."

Velma chatted on as they followed her outside.

"Just follow that path and go past the smaller cabins." She smiled. "You've missed dinner, but I've put a tray of snacks and cold-cuts in your cabin."

"Thank you, Velma." Jenna smiled.

"Don't leave any food out on the deck, or it'll attract the bears."

"Got it," Jenna said. "You have a beautiful place here."

The older woman beamed. "Enjoy. And don't forget to leave a review online."

Park followed Jenna, carrying their bags. Enchanting redwood cabins faced the lake, and they continued past them. The faint strains of country music came from one of them.

The honeymoon cabin was made of logs, had a large deck out front and was bigger than the other cabins. As they walked onto the deck, he spotted two chairs and a table facing the lake. He turned, and for a second, his brain just went empty.

Beside him, Jenna stilled. "Wow."

The view of the lake was breathtaking. Smooth, still water was framed by pristine mountains. Trees surrounded the lake and went part way up the mountains, stopping at the timberline. The tops of the mountains were bare—where trees couldn't grow and the alpine plants took over.

"Nice little spot," he said.

"It sure is. Except I'm guessing winter must be a different story." Jenna took a deep breath of fresh air, then turned and unlocked the front door.

The interior of the cabin was what he'd call rustic luxury. The walls were wood, and there was a small living area with a table, comfy couch, and a small TV. He guessed no one came to Drifter Lake Lodge to sit in their cabin and watch television. He walked through to the bedroom and jerked to a halt.

There was only one bed.

It was huge and made from hewn logs, and covered with white covers and a mound of pillows. There was a fluffy, brown blanket across the bottom.

He'd be sharing a bed with Jenna.

The bags slipped from his hands and hit the floor.

She stepped up beside him. "There's a tray of food in the living area and a coffee machine. Let's eat." She eyed the bed, then him. "It's a big bed, Conroy. We'll manage just fine."

She turned and looked out the picture window.

From the look on her face, he didn't think she was taking in the pristine lake.

"Tomorrow, we'll hike to the hunting cabin and find Olson."

Park nodded. "We will."

JENNA WOKE UP FEELING GREAT. She was warm and snug, and she'd slept like a rock.

Then she froze.

She was in a big, comfy bed, with a hard arm locked around her middle, and a hard, male body curved around hers.

Oh, God.

She and Parker had gone to sleep last night on opposite sides of the large king-size bed, but during the night, they'd obviously met in the middle.

He was big and hot behind her and—she swallowed—there was hard cock digging into her ass.

Tingles zinged down her body. He shifted and she realized his face was buried in her hair, and his big hand splayed on her belly, under the pajama shirt. Her tiny pajama shorts were riding low.

Desire, hot and urgent, pooled between her thighs.

She should extricate herself, even if a part of her didn't want to. She shifted a tiny bit, and his arm tightened. He hauled her even closer. As he shifted, his erection rubbed against her, and she swallowed a moan.

Then she felt him wake up. His body went taut and his fingers flexed on her skin.

Her heart drummed, and when he moved again, his cock pressed even harder against her.

"*Shit*," he muttered.

"That about covers it," she murmured.

They stayed there, locked in a little cocoon. Neither one of them moved.

Then he pulled in a breath and started to move his hand away.

Jenna grabbed his thick wrist, and he froze. Her heartbeat echoed in her head. *Thump. Thump. Thump.* It beat in time with the pulse of desire between her legs.

She wasn't going to lie to herself. She was attracted to Parker Conroy. Big time.

They were hunting a dangerous fugitive. She knew they could get hurt, or worse. Every day, she gave her all for sometimes what felt like very little in return. Her job was rewarding, but also demanding. She did it for a lot of reasons, some of which were tangled up with her father.

Why not finally have something she wanted? Just for a little while.

Something they both wanted.

She pushed his hand lower.

Parker didn't miss a beat. His hand slid into her pajama shorts and panties. Then his fingers were parting her.

"You sure?" his voice was low.

"Yes. Very sure. Touch me, Park."

He stroked her folds and made a low, hungry sound. With a gasp, she arched into him, and let her thighs fall apart.

"So damn soft and slick," he whispered in her ear.

She should be embarrassed about how wet she was, but she wasn't. It felt too good. He found her clit and she moaned.

God.

He took his time, playing with her, stroking her. It was like he was memorizing every inch of her. Then one thick finger pushed inside her. She writhed on his clever fingers and moaned. Her fingers dug into his arm. *"Park."*

"You feel so good, Jenna." He pressed his face to her hair, his breathing uneven, his breath hot on her neck. "Haven't touched something so pretty, so good, in a long time." He worked his finger in and out of her until all she could feel was pleasure. She couldn't think at all.

"Park," she cried.

His hand moved, and she gripped his wrist.

"Don't stop." Her voice was breathless.

"No plans to stop. This sweet pussy is so wet for me."

His voice was low and gritty. Her belly clenched. He pushed another finger inside her, and made her feel the stretch. Then, with a curse, he shoved her shorts and panties down her legs, and she felt his hard cock throb against her ass.

For a second, his hand slid up under her pajama top and cupped one of her breasts. He pinched her nipple, and she let out a husky cry. Then his hand was gone, delving back between her legs. His fingers were back inside her, thumb on her clit, working her hard.

Now she was making desperate little sounds, her legs restless.

"You're getting close," he murmured. "I can't wait to watch you come, Jenna." He stroked deeper, his thumb pressing on her clit. "Come on my fingers. Let me hear you."

She couldn't hold back. She arched, pleasure exploding inside her. Her climax burst—hot and bright. So good. So damn good.

When she came back to reality, pleasure was a low hum in her blood and she was still breathless.

Park was still tense behind her. His cock felt even bigger, still pressing hard against her ass. There was a voice in her head yelling that she shouldn't have done this. Shouldn't have crossed this line.

She ignored it.

She wasn't going to leave him like this. If there was one thing Jenna valued, it was fairness. She spun, her hands pushing at his boxer shorts.

"Jenna—"

"I want to touch you." She met his gaze. "Is that okay? Can I touch your cock, Park?'

He swallowed. "Yes. Fuck, yes."

She took his cock in both hands and stroked. He was long, with a lot of girth.

"Is this okay?" she asked.

Something flashed in his eyes. "Yeah, it's okay. More than okay."

She ran a finger down a thick vein on one side of his cock, liking the way his muscles tensed. Then she pumped him, and his groan filled the room.

She kept working him, and pre-come beaded on the swollen head. She ran her fingers through it.

That earned her a tortured groan. She met his gaze and found it locked on her, unblinking. The muscles in his neck were taut. She stroked harder. God, she wanted him in her mouth.

On the next stroke, his body locked, and she heard his fierce growl. "Coming. Jenna, *fuck*."

She didn't let go. She squeezed, and his release spurted on her fingers and hit her bare belly. His groan was low and sexy.

Finally, he sagged back on the bed. His dark gaze was on her, his eyelids hooded, his chest rising and falling fast.

She swallowed. She suddenly felt stripped of her defenses, her rock-solid control soft and crumbling. This man affected her like no one had before, and she wasn't sure she liked it.

"I think we both needed that." She scooted to the edge of the bed. "It was good stress relief."

"Stress relief?" He sat up.

He looked so big and male, and she had to drag her gaze off him. "Yes, stress relief."

He gripped her chin. "It was more than that and you know it." His head lowered.

"No kissing," she said. "It's too intimate." She couldn't risk getting any closer to this man.

Couldn't risk making another mistake.

He arched a brow. "Me fingering you until you came wasn't intimate?" His voice lowered. "Me coming all over you isn't intimate?" His gaze dropped to her bare belly, looking at his come smeared on her skin.

78

"Look, we're attracted to each other. And it's running pretty hot. I think trying to avoid it will only make it worse. So why not enjoy things while we can? Think of this as colleagues with benefits. I won't be here long, and this is a tough, stressful situation." She rose. "That work for you?"

He was quiet for a beat. "Yeah, that works for me."

Her belly did a funny flutter but she wasn't going to analyze why. "Good."

He made a sound, and when she glanced back, he was staring at her.

"Park?" She tried to dredge up some dignity even though she had no panties on and her legs felt like Jell-O.

His gaze flicked to hers and she swallowed her gasp. It was searing hot.

"I like seeing my come marking your skin."

His words were like an arrow of lust to her core. She swallowed.

Find some control, Jenna. Keep things casual.

"I'm going to take a shower. You can have it after me. We need to get ready for our hike and to find Olson."

She spun, but she felt his gaze on her as she walked into the bathroom.

She needed to keep her head in the game, but Parker made it hard. She closed the door and pressed her forehead against the cool wood.

You have a job to do. Don't let anything get in the way. Her mind was onboard, but her body was a different story.

CHAPTER EIGHT

T he sun was warm on his skin as he hiked along the
trail.

They were about an hour out from the lodge. From
this vantage point, the lake looked even more amazing.
Like something from a postcard.

Park breathed deeply. He could almost believe he
was just on a relaxing hike. Then his gaze sliced to the
woman hiking ahead of him.

Jenna moved with sure steps. She was wearing a pair
of tiny khaki shorts that showed off her toned legs. Her
hair was in a braid and glinted like gold.

She hadn't mentioned the hot, sexy moment they'd
shared this morning. She'd been all business ever since
they'd started the hike.

Stress relief. Colleagues with benefits. He should be
fucking thrilled to hear that. Who didn't want hot sex
without the strings attached?

He had no idea why her words bothered him so
much. He scowled. He should be grateful that he actu-

ally wanted her to touch him. When her hands were on him, all he thought about was her. And pleasure.

Forcing himself to stop thinking about her, he scanned around. The last thing they needed was to run into a damn bear. They should be making more noise, but they didn't want to let Olson know they were coming.

Wild bear or sadistic murderer. Not much of a choice.

A few minutes later, Jenna stopped. She pulled her backpack off her shoulders and pulled out a water bottle. "Drink break."

He lifted his chin and pulled his own water out. A moment later, she handed him a protein bar.

"According to the map, the trail gets a little steeper and rockier from here." She pointed up the hill. "The hunting cabin is up that way."

Parker ate the protein bar in three bites. "Then let's keep moving."

They trekked on.

As they moved through a thicker patch of trees, he suddenly heard movement off to their left. He held up a hand. Jenna froze.

Don't be a damn bear. He slid his hand around his backpack, ready to pull out the bear spray he had clipped to it.

More noise, twigs snapping. Then a large body stepped out of the trees.

Holy shit. The moose idly made its way through the trees. It was huge. It had a glossy brown coat and a massive set of antlers. Park glanced back and saw Jenna's mouth drop open.

The majestic animal didn't appear agitated. It kept

walking, giving no indication it cared about their presence. He knew aggressive moose could charge, but this one kept walking and soon disappeared into the trees.

The tense muscles in his shoulders relaxed.

"Oh my God." Jenna let out a breathy laugh. "I had no idea it would be that big."

"Me neither. I've seen plenty of caribou but not any moose up close."

They shared a smile.

Jenna tightened her braid. "Glad it wasn't a bear."

"Me too." Park set off in the direction of the cabin again.

It wasn't long before he spotted the wooden structure. It was a simple, square building, with no frills. The ground around the cabin was rocky, with few trees.

Jenna and Park paused, carefully surveying the area.

"No sign of movement," she murmured.

"Be careful." Olson wouldn't announce his presence. "I suggest we circle around and check the back."

They did a loop of the cabin. There was still no sign of anyone. They reached the front door and Jenna opened it carefully.

There wasn't anyone inside.

Park took in the canvas cots lined up against one wall, for hunters to sleep on with their sleeping bags. There was a built-in wooden table and bench, and a black, cast-iron woodstove.

"The dust's been disturbed." Park toed the floor with his boot, studying the scrape marks. "Someone was here."

"It could've been anyone."

Then he spotted a perfect shoe print. "Look. It's from an Anvil tactical hiking boot."

"The same custom boots Olson has." She smiled grimly. "He was here. We're on the right track." She glanced around. "Let's look around outside again."

They went out the front door, and Park frowned. He didn't get the impression Olson had stayed here long. He'd come here, then left.

Why? Did he feel too exposed?

Park turned and saw Jenna looking down the hill, lost in thought.

The crack of a gunshot echoed across the valley.

He watched her jerk and slam into the wall of the cabin.

No.

Park leaped. There was another shot, and the bullet hit the dirt nearby. He crashed into Jenna, taking her to the ground. He covered her body with his.

"Jenna. Fuck, *Jenna.*" There was blood on her head.

Another bullet hit the dirt.

"I'm okay." She lifted her hand. "It just clipped me."

Olson had almost shot her in the fucking head. Park's heart raced out of control.

They needed cover.

He lifted off her but stayed low. "Stay down." He grabbed her arm, and they crawled around the side of the cabin and around the back.

There were two more shots, and a window shattered.

"He must have a sniper rifle." Park scowled. "He fired the shots from far away."

Jenna leaned back against the cabin. Blood was dripping down the side of her head.

There were no more gunshots.

"Inside." He helped her up, then smashed his elbow through the window at the back of the cabin. "We need to stay out of view."

He cupped his hands and gestured for her to use it as a step. He helped her climb through the window, then he followed her through.

She crawled over to the wall and leaned against it. He hated seeing the blood on her head. If that shot had been a fraction the other way, she'd be dead.

A dark emotion gripped him, like claws around his throat. Jenna being killed wasn't going to happen, dammit. It wasn't a fucking option.

For a second, he was thrust back to another place. He was running toward his fellow soldiers, trying desperately to save them from a bomb.

Then *boom*.

"Park?"

He clicked back into the present.

"Are you all right?" She looked concerned. For him.

With his heartbeat thundering in his ears, he got his shit together and yanked his backpack open. He pulled out a first aid kit.

"Here." He ripped the kit open, then pressed a wad of gauze to her wound. "We need to stop the bleeding."

"Thanks."

He swallowed. "Hold that in place."

He quickly dug into his backpack and pulled out a set

of binoculars. He crawled across the floor of the cabin and moved up below one of the windows.

"Park—"

"I'll be careful." He rose on his knees and looked out. Based on the shots, he guessed Olson's general area. Through the binoculars, he scanned the far hillside. Nothing. All he could see were trees. But Parker knew Olson was there. Somewhere.

There.

He caught the glint of sunlight shining off something. "Got him."

"He was waiting for us," she said grimly.

Park glanced at her, his gaze moving to the blood-stained cloth in her hand. That damn blood. He turned back to the window and looked through the binoculars again.

The telltale glint was gone.

"I think he's gone, but we need to stay down and still for a bit longer, just in case."

She nodded and sighed. She lowered the gauze, then touched a finger to her head gingerly. "I'd really hoped we'd find him here."

"Well, we did. He's in this area. We're a step closer." Park's gaze moved to her wound. There was a small furrow on the side of her head.

She'd almost died.

His chest was tight and it hurt to draw a breath. He looked out the window again.

Olson would pay for this. Park vowed it.

I'm coming for you, asshole.

ANNA HACKETT

IT WAS late afternoon when they hiked back, and Jenna saw the Drifter Lake Lodge up ahead. It gleamed like a welcoming beacon.

She'd done her best to clean her head wound, but it was stinging. She wasn't going to tell Park. She glanced over at him.

He'd been tense and edgy the entire hike back. She'd felt the contained energy boiling inside him.

Every time he glanced at her head, a muscle ticked in his jaw. He was really mad that she'd gotten hurt. No doubt it brought up some bad moments for him.

He hadn't said much the entire walk back.

She cleared her throat. "Are you all right?"

"No."

When he didn't say anything else, she sighed.

As they neared the lodge, she saw some people on the deck of the main building, having drinks.

"We should probably clean up and make an appearance at dinner. I mean, the newlyweds cover will probably keep people away, but I get the impression that Velma has a need to feed people. She'll hunt us down eventually."

Maybe a good meal might help Park settle.

He just grunted.

She followed him into their cabin.

"I'm going to shower first," she told him. Then she needed to update Owen.

Park nodded, going to check his phone.

Jenna took a quick shower and carefully washed her

86

head wound. It stung like hell. She dried off and looked in the mirror. She had a small groove just past her temple. Park was right, she was lucky as hell. She was probably going to be missing some hair.

She set her shoulders back. Still, she wasn't going to dwell on it. She was alive and that was all that mattered.

The risk was worth it to catch Kyle Olson.

Wrapping the towel securely around her body, she headed into the bedroom. There was no sign of Park. Suddenly, her cellphone started ringing and she snatched it up.

"Hi, Owen."

"Just checking in. No sign of Olson in my area."

"I was about to call you." She sat on the bed. "We had an interaction with Olson."

"You saw him? Where?"

"We didn't see him. Park and I hiked up to a hunting cabin. He wasn't there, but he took a few shots at us with a sniper rifle. It's nothing, but one shot clipped me."

Silence. "Are you all right? Jesus, do you need medical attention?"

"I'm fine, Owen." She didn't need another overprotective male. "It's a graze."

"Where?"

She ran a hand through her damp hair and prodded the edge of the wound. "I'm all right."

"Where, Jenna?" His voice hardened.

"Side of my head. It's nothing."

Owen cursed. "A bullet to the head is not nothing."

"We're getting close. I need you to contact the other

search parties. Get them to block off any routes out of my area and close in. We aren't letting Olson get away."

"I'm coming to you. You need me."

"I have Park."

"Yeah, well, where was he today?"

"Knocking me down and covering me with his own body. Ensuring we got into cover."

Owen's harsh release of breath echoed on the line.

"Stick to the plan, Owen. I've got this."

He sighed. "Be careful."

"I will."

"And Jenna, we know Olson is dangerous, but don't forget that Parker is as well."

He ended the call, and she set the phone on the bedside table. Park still hadn't appeared, and she wondered where he was.

She moved toward the window and that's when she saw him. Swimming in the lake.

Leaning her forehead against the cool glass, she watched his strong strokes. He owned the water, moving with strength and skill. Yes, he was dangerous, but she knew he wasn't a danger to her physically.

She watched until he climbed out and grabbed a towel, running it over his wet chest. He was only wearing a pair of black swim shorts. He walked toward the cabin.

As he stepped inside, he was still damp. She saw beads of water on his skin.

When he saw her, his hand balled into a fist.

Clearly the swim hadn't helped him cool off.

"Park? Talk to me."

"He almost put a bullet in your head." Park's tone was lethal.

She hitched her towel tighter and moved closer. "But he didn't. He missed, and you got me into cover. Almost doesn't count."

"It was too damn close."

"I'm not letting there be a next time. I'm bringing the asshole in, one way or another."

Park's jaw worked. "What if next time...?"

She shook her head and pressed her hands to his damp chest. She saw his cut and noted that it was healing nicely. There was so much tension pumping off him. "What if the next time we nail his ass? My plan is to drag him away in cuffs and put him away for the rest of his life."

"I watched good soldiers die. I wasn't fast enough... and I saw a bomb blast tear them apart."

Her heart clenched. "I'm sorry, Park. Your Ghost Ops teammates?"

He swallowed. "No. I was temporarily attached to a regiment in Afghanistan to help them on a particular mission. The rest of my Ghost Ops team were on another mission in the next province." He released a harsh breath. "Those soldiers were so damn young. They joined the Army to pay for college and to have an adventure." He gripped her wrists. "I can't watch you die, Jenna."

She lifted her chin. "I'm not planning to. I'm made of tough stuff, and we make a good team, Park. I know that together we can take Olson down. Are you with me?"

His chest heaved, then he gave her a clipped nod.

"Good." Because she couldn't help herself, she

kneaded her fingers against his muscles. She felt some of his scars under her fingertips, but she realized she barely saw them. They were a part of him, but not all of him. Mostly, she noted that he was still so tense. "What will help you?"

He cocked his head.

"What will help you let this go? I want to help you feel better."

His gaze flicked up to her wound. "Taking care of your injury."

She moved and sat on the bed, then she waved at her head. "It's all yours. I need it covered for dinner anyway."

He grabbed the first aid kit, then knelt in front of her. Jenna felt flutters start in her belly. He was so close, and she was only wearing a towel.

Park methodically opened the first aid kit. He was so focused as he leaned up and cleaned her wound. She ignored the sting, waiting patiently as he pressed a bandage over it.

"It'll scar," he said.

She shrugged. "I don't care."

His gaze met hers. There was still so much boiling in it.

She swallowed and licked her lips. "I want you to let the darkness go. Don't let it fester. I'm all right. I promise."

"I need more."

Her pulse skipped. "Okay. More what?"

His hands ran up her bare thighs. Electric sensations ignited all over her skin and she sucked in a breath.

"I want to touch you."

"Okay," she whispered.

"I need to hear you cry out my name."

Oh. Goosebumps peppered her skin.

His fingers gripped the towel and hesitated.

Her throat felt thick. When he looked at her, she nodded.

He parted the towel. Another inch and he'd see her bare pussy. She licked her lips, desire roaring to life inside her.

"You going to let me touch you?" His voice was low and gritty. "Wherever I want?"

"Take what you need, Park."

He moved so fast it was shocking. He pushed her back on the bed, then ripped the towel from her body.

All that intensity was focused on her. Right then, she knew nothing else existed for him but her. It was an intoxicating feeling.

He shoved her legs apart, his warm breath ghosting over her stomach, then he moved lower.

Without any warning, his mouth was on her.

There was no preamble, no foreplay. His stubble scraped her inner thighs and he lapped at her with long strokes.

She arched up. "*Park.*"

"*Yes.* That's what I want to hear."

Jenna moaned, her blood going hot. He explored her slick flesh, his hot tongue sliding through her pussy. Her hips lifted and she rocked against his mouth. One of his hands slid under her ass, gripping her hard.

The hungry way he licked and sucked told her how much he liked the taste of her. She panted, feeling her impending orgasm gathering, trying to keep some control.

"You taste so good, Jenna. Sweet, spicy." He licked her like he'd never get enough of her.

God, it felt good. She lifted her hips up to his mouth, making incoherent sounds.

Then he sucked on her clit, pulling it between his lips.

Every muscle in her body was taut. His tongue shifted, delving deep, and he made an appreciative sound. His tongue found her clit again, moving faster. Her hips were moving, her thighs shaking. He sucked on her clit again and it pushed her over the edge.

She broke. She cried out his name, the tension in her exploding into waves of intense pleasure. Her body shuddered.

Jenna flopped back on the bed, feeling like a big pile of goo. Well-pleasured goo.

Park gently nipped her thigh. "Thank you."

She gave a small laugh. "Park, I should be thanking *you* after that." She grabbed his hand. "You okay?"

With a nod he rose. He paid no attention to the large erection tenting his shorts. "I'll go and get ready for dinner." He shot her a small smile, then headed for the bathroom.

She flopped back on the bed again. Her heart hammering in her chest.

That smile. She looked at the ceiling. Not one bit of this felt casual.

Yes, she was in so much trouble. She'd just crossed

another line. Hell, she'd leaped across it willingly. This was already more than she could handle.

She should be focused on her job—her *dangerous* job —not this scarred former soldier. But the truth was, she was worried there was nothing she could do to get her mind off Parker Conroy.

No, that was a lie.

The truth was, she didn't want to get her mind off him.

CHAPTER NINE

V elma had outdone herself.

Sitting at the long, wooden table in the dining room, Jenna glanced out through the doors to the deck. A gentle breeze was blowing in from the lake. It carried some crisp coolness and ruffled her hair. She'd worn her hair down, something she rarely did, and wore a pretty, stretchy headband that hid her injury.

She looked back at the table. Colorful wildflowers sat in small, glass vases, adding a pop of color and whimsy. The rest of the surface was filled with platters and plates of food. There were three different salads, roasted chicken, salmon mac and cheese, and a delicious, slow-cooked, lamb dish.

Around her, all the guests were happy and laughing. The guy from Australia was hilarious, with outrageously funny stories from all his travels.

A new family had arrived that day. They had a daughter who was about five, with long, black hair, and big, blue eyes. Her name was Olivia. She was sitting on the other side of Parker, clutching her doll and jabbering away to him.

"We're going to kayak on the lake tomorrow," Olivia's mother said to the Norwegian couple on the other side of the table.

Jenna shifted on her chair and sensation skittered up her legs. She had stubble burn on her inner thighs and she was sensitive everywhere. She grabbed a water glass and sipped.

Her belly did a flip flop. She was trying not to be drawn to Park more than she already was, but it seemed her body wasn't listening to her head.

If this kept up...

No, she wasn't going to fall for Parker Conroy. She wasn't going to fall for anyone.

One, he didn't want that. Two, her life was elsewhere. She'd capture Olson and then she'd be gone. Three, she didn't trust love at all.

She'd loved her father...and he'd been a monster. She'd never seen it, and at first hadn't believed he was capable of the things he'd done. But he'd fooled them all.

She ate a little more food off her plate, trying to shove all the churning thoughts and emotions away.

Focus on your job, Jenna. They were heading back out looking for Olson tomorrow. That was her main focus.

Her chest tightened. They had to find him, sooner rather than later.

She ate the last bite of her bread roll. *Mmm.* The rolls were homemade and so good. She had a serious weakness for bread.

Park was still talking with Olivia. Without looking at Jenna, he reached out and put his bread roll on her plate.

She stared at it, then at him. She snatched up the roll and tore a piece off.

"Do you like kayaking, Con?" Olivia asked.

"Kayaking? Yeah, it's fun."

The little girl leaned in and whispered. "But...I'm scared of what's in the water. Like a monster, or an evil mermaid octopus witch."

It took Jenna a second to realize it was a reference to the sea witch from *The Little Mermaid*.

"The water's dark," Olivia whispered. "I can't see the bottom."

"I promise you there's just a few fish in there," Park said. "There's nothing that can hurt you."

"You promise, Con?"

"I promise. Think about the fun things, not the things that worry you. Like gliding on the water, enjoying the sunshine, seeing the wildflowers."

The little girl beamed at him. "I like flowers."

Jenna's heart melted as she ate more bread. He was so good with her. For a second, she had the image of Park holding a little girl in his strong arms. One with blonde hair and his dark eyes.

Jeez. She choked on a bit of bread. He turned and thumped her back.

"Thanks," she wheezed.

"You got to chew, chew, chew, Jenna," Olivia said. "That's what mommy tells me."

Jenna swallowed, her throat tight. "Good advice."

Velma came around, clearing away empty plates. Her husband, Ross—a tall, lanky man of few words—helped.

"Dinner was so good, Velma," Jenna said. "Thank you."

The older woman smiled. "You're very welcome. I hope you've left room for dessert."

Soon, Velma brought out homemade chocolate cake and ice-cream. Olivia bounced in her seat.

As the guests all got busy serving dessert, Jenna spotted Velma talking with Ross in hushed tones. The woman's smile was gone and her brow was creased.

Jenna rose and headed over. "Is everything okay?"

"Oh, I'm sure it's nothing, dear." Velma waved a hand. "Some friends of ours, who live in a cabin nearby, were supposed to come down to collect supplies this afternoon. The floatplane came in with fresh supplies today." She nibbled on her lip. "But our friends didn't arrive. I'm guessing they probably got held up."

Prickles broke out on the back of Jenna's neck. "Did you try calling them?"

"Yes, but they only have a satellite phone. There was no answer." Velma wrung her hands. "We can go a while without talking to Tom and Sheryl, but they've never missed a check-in before."

"Where do they live?" Jenna asked.

Velma stepped over to a map on the wall. Drifter Lake was in the center. "Here, on this mountain. They're such a lovely couple."

Jenna patted the woman's shoulder. "I'm sure they're fine. Maybe they had car trouble, like we had."

"That could be it." Velma brightened. "I bet they'll be in tomorrow. We'll have a laugh about it."

Jenna managed a smile. She went back to the table, then leaned into Parker. "A couple who live in the hills near here, friends of Velma and Ross, didn't show up today as expected."

His face sharpened. "Shit. Have you got their location?"

She nodded.

"Good. We'll leave first thing in the morning and check on them."

"From the looks of their cabin, we can drive most of the way, then go in the last little bit on foot. I'll try and get a bit more info about them."

After they'd finished dessert, Jenna chatted with Velma about her friends a little more. The rest of the guests started drifting back to their cabins, and so did Jenna and Parker.

Every step of the way, she prayed that Olson had nothing to do with Tom and Sheryl Hoskins. Jenna wished she could go and check on the couple right now, but it was too dangerous to try and make the trip to their cabin at night.

Tomorrow, she was sure they'd find the Hoskins and they'd be just fine. This was nothing.

The honeymoon cabin came into view and nerves ignited. She and Park were going to share a bed again.

When she stepped inside the cabin, Park didn't follow.

He slid his hands into his pockets. "I want to do a

circle of the lodge grounds, make sure there's no sign of Olson."

"He's unlikely to come here."

"I know, but...there's a little girl here. You're here. I need to."

She nodded, then grabbed his arm. She realized that he no longer tensed up when she touched him. "Be careful."

He inclined his head then disappeared into the growing darkness.

Back in the bedroom, Jenna changed into her pajamas and climbed into bed. She propped herself up on the pillows and figured she'd wait for Park.

But tiredness hit hard, and she found herself finding it harder to keep her eyelids open.

She was sure Park would be back soon.

PARK DID another loop of the lodge grounds.

This was where he did his best work. Alone in the shadows. He paused under a tree, his gaze looking at the way the moonlight hit the lake.

There was no sign of Olson.

Park's gaze shifted to the honeymoon cabin. To Jenna.

The warm glow of a light shone in the windows. Beckoning him.

Shit. He looked down and dragged in some cool night air. He was no good for her. He should never have touched her, let alone put his mouth on her.

Her sweet cries echoed in his ears.

Damn. And now he was hard.

He spun and forced himself to do another loop of the main lodge. He couldn't forget how close Olson had come to killing her today.

I am going to stop you, Olson. I won't let you hurt her again.

In his pocket, his cellphone vibrated. He pulled it out and saw Vander's name on the screen.

"Vander."

"How's the hunt? Have you found him?"

"We're close." Park turned and headed back toward the cabin. "He took a shot at us today. Fucking grazed Jenna's head."

Vander cursed. "She all right?"

"Yeah."

"He must be worried if he's trying to take her out."

"Well, I'm *not* going to let that happen."

Vander was quiet for a beat. "Sounds personal."

Park didn't respond.

"Knew you'd like her. She's tough, smart, and doesn't take any shit. Figured if anyone could get through that hard shell of yours, it would be Jenna."

"I'm not in the market for a woman," Park growled. "You know that."

"Sometimes, you don't choose, Park. When the right woman comes along, she makes you feel things, whether you want to or not. Believe me, I know."

There was a warm note to Vander's usually cool voice, and Park knew the man was thinking of his wife.

"I...you know I don't like being touched. What

happened to me..." He didn't need to share the gory details with his friend.

"You telling me you don't like Jenna touching you?"

Park reached the deck of the cabin, his jaw working. He couldn't lie. "Dammit, I like her touching me too much."

"Good." Vander sounded pleased. "Keep her safe, Park. And watch your back, although I suspect Jenna will do that for you."

"Yeah."

"And if you need me, you call me. You haven't been very good at that lately. You don't need to do everything alone."

Park looked into the darkness. "I'll...try."

"Keep me updated."

"Will do. Thanks, Vander." He opened the door and tucked the phone away.

The cabin was quiet. He walked into the bedroom and came to a halt.

Jenna was asleep, propped up on the pillows. She'd been waiting for him. Gritting his teeth, he moved closer. The blanket was only half covering her, and he saw those tiny sleep shorts that barely covered anything.

He laid her down, throwing some pillows on the floor. She turned on her side and let out a contented noise. He could smell that floral scent of hers and his cock stirred.

He made himself walk away. In the bathroom, he brushed his teeth on autopilot. Back in the bedroom, he stripped down to his boxer shorts and climbed onto his side of the bed. He put a pillow between them.

Then he laid down and stared at the ceiling, surrounded by the tempting scent of Jenna and the soft sound of her breathing.

PARK WOKE up with an armful of warm, sleeping woman.

He closed his eyes and breathed in the scent of Jenna's hair.

The pillow he'd put between them was nowhere in sight, now. Jenna was sprawled half over him, her cheek to his chest. He felt her warm breath puff on his skin. Her hair was loose, and made him think of spun gold.

If she woke up, she'd feel his hard cock poking into her belly.

He stared at the ceiling and tried to dredge up some control. He was already sliding in too deep with her. Yesterday, seeing her hurt and coming so close to being killed, had rattled him.

Hell, the only thing that had calmed him was throwing her on the bed and hungrily eating her pussy like a wild man.

His cock throbbed at the memory and he swallowed a groan. He didn't want to care. He didn't want to feel.

He shifted, but she made a sleepy sound that went straight to his dick. He was rock hard.

She shifted, then pressed a kiss to his chest.

He jolted. Sleepy blue eyes looked up at him. She shot him a lazy smile, then peppered kisses along his chest, and without hesitation, across his scars.

"Jenna..."

"Shh." Slowly, she moved lower. She pressed a quick kiss to his healing cut.

His hands twisted in the sheets. God, this was torture of the best kind. It had been so long since he'd enjoyed anyone touching him.

She took her time, kissing and nipping. She bit his abs, and his muscles contracted.

Then, she pushed his boxers down and his hard cock sprang free.

Jenna made a sound. "I wanted this in my mouth yesterday."

Before he could say anything, she wrapped her mouth around his cock and swallowed him deep.

He cursed, his hips bucking up.

Her hot tongue pressed against him. Her hand slid to the base of his cock, holding him as her head bobbed.

"Jenna, *fuck*. So good." He had to fight from coming straight away.

Looking down, he watched her sucking him, her cheeks hollowing. She took him as deep as she could, making a little hum of pleasure.

He wanted to thrust deep, wanted to fuck her sweet mouth.

Her gaze met his and she sucked harder.

Park's willpower tore like paper. "Suck me, Jenna."

She did. Taking him deeper.

He cupped her jaw, his thumb sliding over her skin. "You like my cock in your mouth? You like the way I taste?"

For an answer, she moved faster.

He groaned, his hips thrusting forward. "Fuck. I'm going to come." His hand slid into her hair. "You going to swallow for me?"

Jenna didn't let up, just nodded as she worked his cock with her mouth.

"I'm coming." With a deep groan, he came, shooting his release into her mouth. She kept sucking, swallowing it all down.

"*Jesus.*" He was out of breath, like he'd run ten miles with a heavy pack.

Jenna eased her mouth off his cock and rose. She smiled, her blonde hair spilling around her face. "I'm going to get ready. We need to get going."

He grabbed her wrist, and her gaze met his.

He wanted to say something, but he didn't know what.

She winked at him and slid off the bed.

Casual. They were keeping this casual. He couldn't let himself forget that. He pinched the bridge of his nose. That was what he wanted.

He had to keep reminding himself of that.

Forty minutes later, they were both dressed and in the Tahoe.

"The Hoskins, Tom and Sheryl, are both former corporate executives from Chicago," Jenna said. "They burned out from working long hours and decided to retire to Alaska. They built an off-grid cabin."

Park navigated a bumpy section of road. "Let's hope they're just sick, or their vehicle broke down."

She nodded. There were lines bracketing her mouth, and he knew that she was worried.

They reached the end of the trail.

"We walk from here," she said.

After he'd parked the SUV, they both pulled on their backpacks. Then, they set off into the trees.

The Hoskins had picked a nice spot. They came to the edge of the tree line. Park took in the cute A-frame cabin, made of a rich, dark wood. Glass windows faced the view into the valley.

It was quiet. He scanned their surroundings. "No vehicle."

"There's nothing," Jenna said, her voice low.

No one came to greet them. There were no animal noises.

She started toward the cabin, and he followed her. His instincts were pinging hard. Something was wrong.

"There's a small garage at the back." Jenna pointed. "Their car must be in there."

She continued toward the front of the cabin. A ring of rocks forming a fire pit sat nearby with two wooden chairs beside it.

"Stop!" He grabbed her and yanked her back.

She stumbled into him. "What's wrong?"

"Something's off." He didn't know what, he just knew he'd had to stop her.

She cocked her head. "It's those spidey senses you have, isn't it?"

"I'm not a damn superhero." He caught the glint of something right at her feet. "Don't move." He crouched.

There was a long, thin wire at knee height, strung between two trees.

"Hell," Jenna murmured.

Park followed the string to the closest tree. He saw the grenade taped to the bark.

Now she cursed. "God, if I'd hit that..."

"Olson was here." Park rose. "This is one of his booby-traps. We were trained to make things like this." He looked at the house. "Follow me."

They walked carefully, checking every inch of the ground. When they reached the front deck, Park pulled a flashlight out of his backpack and looked under the steps.

"There's another device attached to the second step." He stepped over it. "Be careful."

Then, he took his time checking the front door.

"It's clear." He tried the handle and the door opened.

There was silence inside.

"Mr. and Mrs. Hoskins?" Jenna called. "US Marshals."

No response.

But a very familiar smell hit Park. And from the way Jenna's face hardened, she smelled it, too.

She pulled her weapon.

The Hoskins' cabin smelled like death.

106

CHAPTER TEN

She walked in, her Glock 22 up, checking every corner.

The cabin was tidy and neat as a pin, with the clean lines of Scandinavian-style décor. The walls were white, with some large mirrors, and cozy blankets were tossed over the beige couch. She walked past the kitchen with its bright, white cabinets and butcher block counter tops. Park was one step behind her, his gun resting easily in his hand. She noted that he carried a Heckler & Koch handgun.

She jerked her head to the hallway, and he nodded.

She didn't stop to dwell on how easily they communicated and worked together. Moving into the short hall, she steeled herself. There was a dropped blanket on the floor, like someone had been startled and dropped it. The scent of death intensified.

Jenna turned through a doorway.

The bedroom was bright and filled with light, the golden glow a dramatic contrast to the destruction within.

A chair had been tipped over, and the debris from several smashed items was littered around the room.

The Hoskins had clearly put up a fight.

Her stomach curdled. It didn't matter how many times she saw death, it still affected her. Tom Hoskins was lying on the floor, next to the toppled chair. There was a large, dried pool of blood underneath his head. Strings of rope were attached to the chair, and he'd clearly been tied to it at some stage. He'd died from a gunshot wound.

His wife was on the bed. Her arms were flung out wide and the ligature marks on her neck were obvious.

"Fucking hell," Park muttered.

"Olson did this." Jenna had been too late to stop him. Her chest felt like it was filled with rocks. She stepped closer to the bed. Sheryl had brown hair, with a touch of gray she'd clearly been growing out. Her hair was tangled around her face.

For a second, Jenna had a flashback to another dead woman. Barely more than a girl, with sightless eyes, dried leaves tangled in her brown hair.

"It doesn't look like he raped Mrs. Hoskins," Park said. "She's still dressed."

Jenna looked away, pulling in a short breath. "A small blessing. I think her husband got free and must have surprised Olson."

Park's mouth flattened. "So, he killed Tom, and since he'd lost his audience, he didn't go through with the rape."

No, Olson had just strangled the poor woman to death. The sick bastard.

Anger was a hot ball in her stomach. "I have to call it in to Dunford."

Park didn't respond. He crouched, looking at something on the floor.

"What is it?" she asked.

"Olson got blood on his boots." Park rose and followed the trail to the window. It was wide open. "Come on. Let's see if we can find which direction he went."

Outside, they carefully navigated around another booby trap, and Jenna followed Park as he stared at the ground, heading away from the cabin.

She couldn't see anything, but clearly he could. "You can really tell that he went this way?"

"Yes. I'm trained to look for tracks and signs. I can see the small depressions he's left, even if there isn't a full footprint. Plus, there are some small smudges from the blood."

Park stopped at the tree line. "No more blood, but he was moving in that direction. He's left a few tiny signs. Maybe he didn't think anyone would find the couple. Thought he was safe."

"I need to call this in."

He nodded.

Jenna pulled the satellite phone out of her backpack and called the state troopers. After she'd relayed all the details of the murder and their location, she checked in with Owen.

Since she and Park had spotted Olson yesterday, Owen and the other search teams were closing in to this location. They were trying to make sure Olson didn't slip away if he tried to escape.

Still, Alaska was wild and open, and Olson was good at staying hidden.

I'm going to catch you. No matter what.

When she finished the calls, Park was fiddling with the device on the front steps.

Her pulse jumped. "Park, you'd better not..."

He rose, the grenade in his hand. "I've disabled it. We need to clear the area, and search for any more devices that he might have left behind."

"All right. The troopers are sending a helicopter. Dunford said his team will process the scene." She released a breath. "Those poor people. They left the big city, and ended up being murdered in a remote cabin in Alaska." She shook her head. "Olson can run, but he can't hide forever. I'm going to take great pleasure in taking him down."

"This isn't your fault, Jenna."

She looked at him. "I wasn't fast enough."

"Hey—" he grabbed her arm.

"You know," she said quietly. "You know how this feels. You told me that soldiers you knew died, and that you couldn't save them in time."

His jaw worked. "Yes, but I didn't plant the bomb that killed them. I struggle with the fucking guilt that I made it out, but—" his face twisted "—objectively, I know I did everything I could."

He looked away at the trees. His face was in profile as he dragged in a breath.

Objectively didn't mean squat when the guilt choked

THE HERO SHE LOVES

you. She wondered if he'd spoken to anyone else about the guilt that was eating away at him. She pressed a hand to his back, and his muscles tensed.

They might not be in a relationship, but the two of them were currently tangled up, whether they liked it or not.

"I know this is on Olson," she said. "I'll work through the guilt. And you need to work through yours."

He glanced back at her, that intense gaze on her face. "Something else is driving you." He cocked his head. "This is about your father."

She stepped back. "I'm not talking about him." She swallowed, her throat thick. "Not now. Not here." She lifted her chin. "Let's search for more booby traps."

IT WAS evening when they got back to the Drifter Lake Lodge.

Jenna was quiet and she looked tired, but worse, she was still upset about the couple who'd lost their lives.

She was still blaming herself.

A part of Park was desperate to make her feel better. "You go and shower, and I'll get us some food from Velma."

She nodded tightly and walked into the cabin.

Quickly, he headed to the main lodge. He gave Velma and Ross a bogus story about Jenna having overdone it on the hike and being exhausted. The woman loaded him up with a tray of food.

ANNA HACKETT

As he entered the cabin, he was hit by steamy air and the scent of limes.

Jenna had showered and was wrapped in a big, fluffy robe, her hair still wet. She was sitting on the edge of the bed, staring at nothing.

He set the tray of food on the nightstand.

"Hey." He sat beside her.

"Those poor people. They were just living their lives, not hurting anyone. He killed them. Brutally. He just ended them."

"I told you that it's not your fault."

Sad eyes met his. "But it's not so easy to believe that. It was my job to stop Kyle Olson." She shook her head. "The guilt sneaks up and grabs you by the throat. And it doesn't let go."

"Yeah." It was the perfect description. His hands clenched, then released. He stopped fighting his need to comfort her. He pulled her onto his lap. "Just hold onto me, Jenna."

A sob escaped her, and she quickly turned, straddling him and holding onto him for dear life.

"I don't cry," she said.

"It messes with your tough marshal vibe?" He ran a hand gently up her back. "I won't tell anyone."

"I know. You always tell the truth." She lifted her head. "Don't you?"

"Yeah. Even when it sucks." He cupped her jaw. "Tell me."

She stiffened. "About what?"

"Your father. Why you feel so much guilt. What

drives you to track down the bad guys like it's your own personal crusade."

She sucked in a breath.

For a moment, she didn't say anything, and Park thought he'd pushed too hard. Hell, he'd come to Alaska to avoid spilling his damn personal demons. Now, he was poking at her to share hers.

"Forget it, I..."

"He killed young women. In their late teens and early twenties. I was about nine or ten years old. They weren't much older than me." Her voice was toneless. "We lived in California, near the coast south of San Francisco. He'd pick them up hitchhiking. He seemed like a nice, friendly family man. Safe. They didn't know he was a monster."

Park tensed. "The California Hitchhiker Killer?"

She nodded. "Yes. My father, James Mitchell Sheridan, was a serial killer. He murdered those women and dumped their bodies in the woods, covered in leaves and flowers.

God. What the hell could Park say to comfort her?

"I didn't believe it at first. No ten year old wants to believe the loving father she adores, who takes her to the zoo and buys her candy, is a depraved killer." She shook her head. "My mother didn't believe it at first. But once we saw the evidence, I think she realized it made sense. He was a traveling salesman. He was on the road a lot. He'd been away at the time of every murder, and the police found trophies he'd kept from his victims. Jewelry, ribbons, scarves. He'd hidden them under the floorboards in his study."

"Hell, I'm sorry, Jenna. No kid should have to go through that."

"My mom divorced him and eventually remarried. My stepdad offered for me to take his surname."

"But you didn't."

"No. It was *my* name, and I wanted to make it mean something other than murder."

So she'd become a marshal and dedicated her life to capturing killers like her father. To making amends for crimes that were never hers.

"After I joined the Marshals, I got access to my father's case file. I went over every murder, saw pictures of every victim, and promised I'd get justice for them."

Park tugged her closer. "Jenna, they got justice when he was jailed."

"He was executed four years ago."

"Then justice was well and truly served. Those were *his* crimes to pay for, not yours."

"It never feels like enough," she whispered. "When I saw that poor couple today..." She dashed away her tears. "I hate crying."

She hated appearing weak. What she didn't realize was that it was the opposite.

He ran his thumb across her jaw. Her skin was so soft. "Showing your emotions, rather than locking them up and ignoring them, that's true strength. Trust me, ignoring them is easy."

She just stared at him.

He caught one of her tears. "You'll probably feel better if you get it out."

"I...can't." She swallowed. "The last time I cried, I was ten. I..."

After her entire life had imploded. After the man she'd loved, who'd probably always been the one to comfort her, had turned out to be a monster.

"You can. I've got you, Jenna. Just lean on me."

A tear slid down her cheek, then she broke. She pressed her face to his neck and cried. And he knew she was crying for a dead couple she didn't even know, for her murdered marshals, for her father's victims, and for herself. For that little girl whose life had been shattered. He suspected a few of the tears were for him, too.

He held her and wished he could protect her from everything. Be her shield. He knew she didn't need him to do it, but he still wanted to.

Finally, she sagged against him. Spent.

"Feel better?"

"I do." Her voice was a little scratchy from the crying jag.

"You're the strongest woman I've ever met, Jenna."

Her hands gripped his shoulders and flexed. She lifted her head.

Park's gut tightened. The look in her eyes had changed.

She needed something else now.

"Park..." Her hands cupped his face.

Then her mouth was on his. The kiss was fierce. Her tongue slid into his mouth, stroking his. He pressed his hands to her back, keeping his mouth glued to hers as they devoured each other.

Her robe fell apart and she rocked on his body.

"I need you, Park. I need you so bad."

He growled, tangling a hand in her wet hair. The next kiss was harder, a little savage.

Fuck, he needed her, too.

She bit his lip, and he tasted blood. Her mouth moved across his jaw and cheek, across his scars. She took a second, peppering kisses on the burn scar on his neck.

"*Fuck*. You don't have to—"

She didn't pause. One of her hands snaked under his shirt, fingers rubbing over a knife scar, then another. Next, she found an old bullet scar under his ribs, fingertip circling it.

"These show you survived, Park. To me, they show your strength." Her mouth moved upward, and she bit his earlobe. "I need you to fuck me. Hard."

Desire had claws and they sank deep into his gut.

Her heated blue gaze met his. "If you want that. If you want me."

Want her? The word didn't do justice to the feelings coiling in his gut. He still didn't like the idea of anyone touching him...except Jenna. He exploded off the bed, carrying her across the room and pinned her to the wall. The robe was completely open, showing off her fit body and beautiful breasts.

"You want my cock?"

Her face was flushed, her eyes hot. "*Yes*. Make me feel it."

"I don't have a condom." He shoved her legs apart, pressing closer. He took her mouth hard with his. "I wouldn't use it if I did." He whispered the words hotly against her lips. "I want to feel you. All of you. I want nothing in the way."

She cried out. "Do it."

It was like a primitive part of his brain had taken over. He fumbled with his belt and opened his shorts. She was making needy little sounds.

"Hurry, Park."

He got his cock free. It was so hard it hurt. He shoved her thighs wider and notched the head of his cock in place. Then he slammed home.

She let out a wild cry.

"God..." Sensation rocked through him. It had been so long since he'd been inside a woman, but it had never felt like this. Like he was joined with her.

"Move, Park."

He pulled back and slammed back in.

"*Yes*," she sobbed.

He thrust into her with a punishing rhythm. She needed this. He needed this.

Her fingernails dug into his skin.

"You're so fucking tight, Jenna. You feel so good."

She gasped out his name. "You fill me up."

He angled his hips and when the tone of her cries changed, knew he was hitting the right spot. He knew she was getting close.

"Not deep enough," he growled.

He spun away from the wall, and she cried out in protest. He tossed her on the bed, on her hands and knees. He yanked the robe away and pulled her to the edge. Quickly, he pulled his shirt off and ditched the rest of his clothes.

His gaze traced over her ass. *Perfection.* He pressed a hand to her lower back and the other circled his cock.

He lined up and thrust back into her from behind. She tossed her head back and made a low sound.

Now he was deep enough. He gripped her hips. Their skin slapped together as he thrust inside her. She pushed back against him and her hands twisted in the sheets.

"I love the way you take me," he growled.

She looked over her shoulder, her face flushed and her lips parted. "I can take you. I can take whatever you give me."

He slid a hand under her body and found her clit. "Gonna make you come now. Want to feel the way you come on my cock."

It didn't take long. As he thumbed her clit, she came, screaming his name. Her body clamped ruthlessly down on his cock.

"Fuck. Jenna. *Jenna.*"

With another deep plunge, he came. He felt like a bolt of lightning hit him. He spilled his hot release inside her.

He curled over her body, holding her tight.

There was no noise, no pain, no guilt. Just Jenna.

In that moment, he found something he'd never found before.

Peace.

CHAPTER ELEVEN

"I never pegged you as a man who took baths." Jenna stirred her hand in the warm water, leaning back against Park's hard, naked body.

"I've never taken one before. I don't mind it." He tugged on her hair. "Although I'm pretty sure it's the company I like most."

She smiled. After the most intense sex of her life, she'd been surprised when he'd run a bath for them in the huge tub. Her smile widened. He'd lit a couple of candles but had drawn the line at using bubble bath.

She guessed that was one step too far for a badass former Ghost Ops soldier.

She was pleasantly sore between her legs. The sex had been rough, but exactly what she'd needed. What she'd wanted.

"Open," he said.

She obeyed, opening her mouth, and he fed her some cheese and crackers. He'd brought the tray of food into the bathroom, and he'd been feeding her little bites. The man really liked watching her eat.

He seemed to like looking after her.

Her stomach felt funny. She'd never needed someone to look after her.

After her father had gone to prison, she'd vowed to never need anyone.

She and Park had discussed their lack of protection. Luckily, she used contraception, and had been tested during a physical recently. Park been tested, too, when he'd left Ghost Ops, and he hadn't been with anyone since he'd left the military.

Until her.

Jenna snuggled deeper against his hard chest. Not letting herself think too hard about how much she loved the fact that he liked her touching him.

She'd spilled all her sordid family history...and he'd just listened. He hadn't looked at her any differently. He'd told her she was strong, and everything he'd done showed how much he liked her strength.

Her eyelids closed. She was starting to feel tired now.

"I can track Olson," Parker said.

Jenna sat up and turned to look him. "You're sure?"

"It's worth a try."

They didn't have any better leads right now, unless the state troopers found something in the Hoskins' cabin. But Jenna and Park searched it and all they had was the blood trail Olson had left. "All right. Tomorrow, let's go after him."

"We'll need food, supplies, and camping gear."

And weapons. She nodded. She rested her hand on his thigh and rubbed. "We should get some sleep."

Reluctantly, they got out of the bath and dried off. They needed a decent rest if they were going to hike into the Alaskan wilderness.

She wrapped a towel around her body and listened to the bath water gurgle as she brushed her teeth.

Park pulled on clean, black boxer briefs, and she watched him in the mirror. That body... The hard muscles, the scars. He was every inch the warrior.

Heat sparked in her belly. She'd never run this hot before. How could she want him again after what they'd shared earlier?

She headed out into the bedroom. She dropped the towel and climbed into the bed.

Park watched her and flicked on one of the bedside lamps, then turned the overhead light off. His gaze was on her naked body.

"No pajamas tonight?" he asked.

She shook her head.

He strode to the bed, then shoved his boxer shorts off and kicked them away.

"Then I need to eat that sweet pussy again."

Her heartbeat set off at a breakneck pace. She lay back and let her thighs fall open.

With a growl, he was on her. His hands gripped her thighs, pushing them wide, then his tongue was lapping between her legs.

Jenna's head fell back. Pure pleasure ran through her. He licked and sucked and teased like he couldn't get enough.

She wanted him to feel this pleasure, too.

"Park." She grabbed at him. "Come here."

He looked up and paused, his mouth glistening with her juices. His hungry gaze was on her face.

"Come this way," she said. "Straddle me."

He hesitated, then obeyed. That left him crouched over her, with his head between her legs, and his thighs on either side of her head.

That beautiful cock of his was right in front of her face.

He went back to licking at her clit.

She licked the head of his cock and heard his low groan. The salty taste of him hit her and she sucked him deep. Soon, the room was filled with the sounds of their pleasure. She knew neither of them would last long.

Suddenly, he pulled away.

"*No*," she said.

"Not coming down your throat this time." He spun, and his body came down over hers. He gripped her hands, pinning her arms to the bed above her head. His hips pressed between hers, then without warning, he pushed inside her.

Oh. She arched her body into his. His dark gaze was on her face. This time, his thrusts were deep, but slow.

"*Park*," she murmured, pushing into his hard grip.

He kept her pinned. "Slow this time."

They moved together. She liked him holding her down, and she realized that he was the only man she'd let do that.

Heat built inside her. Their gazes caught and her

breath tangled in her throat. He looked harsh, tough, but she wasn't afraid.

"*Jenna.*" His thrusts got faster, firmer. His hard cock filled her, stretched her. She matched his thrusts, moving into each plunge.

He released her arms, then gripped her legs, and pushed them toward her chest. He went deeper. Possessed her.

Pressure was building inside her. "Park, I—" She broke.

The pleasure burst and rushed over her. She cried out and shuddered through the intense burn of her climax.

He followed her a second later. He thrust deep and groaned her name. She felt the hot spill of his release, then she was too lost in the pleasure to be conscious of anything.

Finally, he rolled onto the bed beside her, his chest heaving. She rolled into him, her face on his chest. She let out a contented sigh.

His big hand cupped her ass, holding her close.

Despite everything, she felt the best she'd felt in a long time.

"Guess you don't mind being touched anymore," she murmured.

He was quiet for a beat. "Only if you're the one touching me."

Her heart swelled. *Oh God.* She wasn't supposed to feel like this. To feel so much for this scarred hero.

"Sleep now," he said.

She nodded, and he reached out to turn off the lamp, plunging them into darkness.

Jenna went to sleep, thinking that being held by Parker Conroy was the best place she'd ever slept.

HE PULLED to a stop on the track to the Hoskins' cabin.

He and Jenna got out of the vehicle. It was still early, soft, morning light bathing the scenery. It made everything look like a delicate, watercolor painting.

But today, they were going to hunt a dangerous killer.

There was nothing soft or delicate about that.

Jenna opened the back of the SUV. Her face was set in serious lines, her hair in a tight braid. There was no sign of the eager lover from last night. His fingers curled into his palms.

Last night... The best night of his life.

He gave his head a quick shake and locked down his feelings. They'd agreed to keep this thing between them casual. As soon as they caught Olson, she'd board a plane and be gone from his life. Like she never existed.

He made himself focus. He had to stay on point today. There was too much at stake.

They were both wearing lightweight hiking pants and boots. They pulled their backpacks on. They had plenty of food, as well as a small, compact tent and basic camping gear. Park had put more in his backpack. He'd been trained to hike for days with a heavy pack.

She looked up. "Let's do this."

With a nod, he set off.

She'd checked in with Owen on the drive up. The marshal and the state troopers were much closer now, ensuring Olson wasn't trying to leave the area. They were on standby, in case Jenna and Parker needed backup.

They fell into an easy hike up the hill. When the cabin came into view, Jenna stopped. He saw the sadness on her face, felt it, but he hoped that the guilt had lessened.

Has yours?

For once, he didn't ignore the voice in his head. Yeah. Maybe it had. Or at least, maybe he was on a path where it would.

He thought of those soldiers who'd died. Some had been so young, but so proud to serve their country. He remembered sharing a beer with Leo. The man had always been a smiling, happy, young guy. And Kristy, who'd been tougher than most of the guys she served with and loved making silly videos to send home to her family.

"At least they're together," Jenna said. "The Hoskins clearly loved each other, and they're together."

He nodded. "You believe in an afterlife?"

"Sure. I believe there's something. Maybe not Pearly Gates and fluffy clouds, but there's something." She pulled in a deep breath, then turned away from the cottage. "Can you pick up the trail?"

Park moved to the spot where he'd seen signs of Olson's escape. He searched and spotted a partial boot print. There was also a small twig and leaf that had been torn off a bush.

"Got it." He set off.

A few times, they had to stop while Park searched to

find the trail. Olson had moved east for a while, then turned to head north. Finally, he'd circled around, moving west.

Once he was some distance from the cabin, he'd stopped working so hard to hide his trail, and it became a bit easier to track him.

As the morning wore on, they stopped for a quick break but kept a fast pace.

Where are you, asshole?

I'm coming for you.

Olson was a blight on Ghost Ops. A blight on humanity. He'd made Jenna cry and almost killed her.

That motivated Park most of all.

He pushed for more speed, striding through the trees.

"Hey, I need a break."

He slowed down and turned. Jenna's face was covered in a sheen of perspiration.

"I get that you can keep this punishing pace up for hours, but clearly I'm not as fit as I thought I was." She pressed her hands to her thighs and bent over.

"Sorry." He'd been moving at a Ghost Ops pace. Hell, she'd kept up with him for a long time. He touched her back. "You're plenty fit. It felt like you were one of my Ghost Ops teammates."

She shot him a look, her lips twitching. "Hopefully none of your Ghost Ops buddies had sucked your cock the night before."

Lightness hit him and he couldn't hold back a laugh. "Hell, no."

She straightened, her gaze on his lips. "That's the first

time I've heard you laugh out loud like that. You have a nice laugh."

He stilled. "It's the first time I've laughed in a long time."

She drank from her water bottle and offered it to him.

"All right, Conroy, I'm ready. But maybe a slightly slower pace this time?"

After a sip of water, he put the bottle back in her backpack.

"Okay." Then he spun her and pressed a quick kiss to her lips.

She smiled up at him. *That smile.* He realized he'd do a lot to keep it on her face.

They set off again, and he was careful to keep a steady pace that looked right for Jenna.

Every step brought them nearer to closing in on Olson.

Soon, the asshole would be locked away. Jenna and the marshals wouldn't make the same mistake twice and let him escape again.

And Park was there to make sure she didn't get hurt while she brought him in.

Whatever happened between Park and Jenna, whatever the future brought, it didn't change his driving need to keep her safe.

It was as strong as his need to serve his country had been.

He glanced at her. He'd give everything to protect her, even his own life, if that's what it took.

CHAPTER TWELVE

I t was tough terrain, but damn beautiful.

Jenna picked her way down the hillside. The panoramic vista stole her breath away. Right now, everything was lush green, but she knew in winter the view would be completely different. Covered in snow, more forbidding, but still gorgeous.

She'd been sending out regular prayers that they wouldn't run into any bears. That was the last thing they needed, especially when their quarry was just as dangerous.

Park was right beside her, but he didn't look tired or like he needed a break. He was incredibly fit. She already knew he had stamina. She smiled, thinking of the previous night.

Then her smile faded.

She was sliding headlong toward... She wasn't exactly sure what, but she had serious feelings developing for this man.

She bit her lip. She was probably signing up for heartbreak. She realized clearly now that Vic had never gotten close to her heart.

Parker...

He could own it.

Except he didn't want it.

He'd made it clear that relationships were not on his radar. He just wanted to avoid people and live in his cabin.

He wanted to avoid life.

She lifted her chin. *No.* For his sake, she wasn't going to let him do that.

Her boot skidded on some loose rocks. She gasped and caught herself.

Park glanced back. "Okay?"

"I'm good." She straightened. "I should warn you, I'm not really that into camping."

"Fresh air. Views. Nature. What's not to like?"

"Bugs. Sleeping on the ground. No bathroom."

He smiled at her. "City girl."

At that moment, a familiar sound caught her ear. She cocked her head.

"There's a river nearby," he said.

They continued down into the valley. A wide river snaked through the narrow gorge. In places, it splashed over rocks—wild and rugged.

The temperature was cooler here and the shadows deeper. She heard a noise and they both spun, pulling out their weapons.

The caribou froze, staring back at them. It looked like something out of a Christmas movie, with its thin antlers and fluffy tail.

"Wow."

At Jenna's low murmur, the deer ran off, disappearing into the trees.

"The caribou are migrating this time of year," Park said.

When she turned back, he was crouched, scowling at the ground.

"What's wrong?"

"I've lost Olson's trail."

"What?" She looked around. "He stopped being careful a long time ago. There has to be something."

"He came to the river here." Park stopped at the river's edge.

Jenna glanced around him and saw a clear boot print. "Did he swim across?"

"I'm not sure. Let's cross the river and take a look on the other side."

They walked upstream to where a large tree had fallen across the river, making a natural bridge. Water rushed underneath it.

With her arms out, Jenna carefully balanced and crossed the log. She knew the water would be cold, and didn't fancy a dip.

Park followed behind her, and soon, he was moving up and down the riverbank, searching for any sign of Olson.

She heard him curse, his frustration clear.

"Hey, let's take a break." She touched his arm.

"We'll lose the good light soon." His mouth flattened and he scanned the trees. "We can't let him get away. I won't let him."

"Hey." She spun Park around.

His face was tight and his body tense. She went up on her toes and kissed him. His mouth opened for her, and the kiss deepened. He slid an arm around her waist and hauled her up against his body.

"You distracted me on purpose," he said.

"You needed it." She stroked his jaw. "Sometimes, we get too lost in the hunt, in the job, in the details. You can lose sight of the bigger picture. Sometimes you need to step back and just take a breath."

"Or kiss a beautiful woman." He tucked a strand of her hair that had escaped her braid behind her ear.

"Well, can't say I've kissed a woman before. Not the way I kiss you." She liked that he thought she was beautiful. She was used to being the smart one, or the tough one.

"Let's take another look now," she suggested.

They followed along the riverbank. Park stopped to study something, and Jenna kept walking.

Then a scent hit her.

Something was dead.

"Park."

He joined her, frowning. "I smell it. I'm guessing a dead animal, maybe."

They followed a bend in the river. The stench increased, and she pressed a hand to her nose.

Then Park grabbed her arm and pulled her to a stop. She followed his gaze, and her stomach did a sickening turn.

There were three animals. They were staked out in the dirt and they'd all been skinned.

"A caribou, a fox, and something else small," Park said. "A marmot, maybe."

"He didn't eat the meat," she said.

"No." Park's face was grim. "Olson did this for fun." He walked over to a fallen log, and she spotted the animals' skins draped over it.

God, Olson was seriously disturbed. He was a psychopath who'd been trained to be the best killer he could be.

"He camped here," Park said.

She glanced over and saw him walking toward the trees.

"Then he went this way." Park motioned ahead.

"So, we keep following him."

"We can't now. We're going to lose the light soon." He turned back to her. "We need to find a spot to make camp."

She pulled a face. "I'm not camping here."

"No, not here. I'll bury the animals, then we'll go up the hill. I want to find a more secure location. I have some portable security cameras that I'll set up. No one will sneak up on us."

"All right. Let's get these poor animals buried, and make camp."

PARK GOT the small tent set up. It wasn't very big. It would be a cozy fit for the both of them.

Darkness was falling fast, as was the temperature. He

circled around the camp, searching for anything that set his radar off.

Nothing.

He pulled out the portable cameras and set them in some tree branches around their camp site. He pulled out his phone and checked the connection to the cameras.

No one was sneaking up on them in the night.

He walked back toward the tent. Jenna was sitting on a log and had a jacket on now. She was opening their food.

"We can't make a fire, but we can use the small propane heater from my backpack," he said.

"Dinner is not going to be up to Velma's standards."

Park sat beside her. "It'll still be better than what I ate most days in the military."

Jenna heated up the food, and passed him a bowl filled with pasta.

He took a mouthful. "Definitely better."

She ate some of her own dinner. She looked lost in thought.

"You all right?" he asked.

She sighed. "So much death. For what? My marshals were good men, with families. Now, they're gone. The Hoskins were innocent. What is so broken in Kyle Olson for him to want to do this?"

"Killing gives him a thrill, some sort of sick pleasure. Maybe he can't feel anything else." Park paused. "I was good at killing. When I left Ghost Ops... I wondered if I was broken."

"You're *nothing* like Kyle Olson, Park."

"For so long, what I did felt right, I had a purpose. I felt I was helping in a way that only I could. I was fighting so others didn't have to. Then after my torture, when I woke up in the hospital..." He touched the scars on his neck. "After that, everything felt wrong. I was alive, and other good men and women weren't. I had nightmares and didn't want anyone to touch me. I was numb and I wanted to stay that way."

"It's not your fault. What you went through, losing your friends. The blame is on the insurgents who killed them." She reached over and touched his neck, her fingers gentle on his scars. "The men who hurt you."

"The guilt. It's so huge sometimes. Those guys were so young, so innocent, in a way. They joined the Army to pay for college, to belong, to have an adventure. It ended in blood."

She took his hand and squeezed.

"You were right. Coming to Alaska...I was running. Vander warned me." Park turned her hand over, entwining their fingers. "Watching you struggle with the guilt over your marshals, grieving for the Hoskins, I guess it made me realize that what I felt was normal. That eventually, I'll work through the guilt and everything else. I couldn't change what happened to my fellow soldiers, couldn't change what happened to me."

"You need to remember them, Park, but you also need to remember that life goes on." Her thumb brushed over his wrist. "Do you want to tell me what happened?"

His chest felt tight. It still hurt to talk about it, but the words welled up inside him.

"Leo was a real character. Always making jokes. Roger was quiet and huge. He had to duck every time he entered a room. And Mitch was the serious, studious one. He liked to game. Kristy was tough as nails and kept the others in line. You'd have liked her."

"Sounds like my kind of person."

"I was only supposed to be attached to their regiment for a few weeks. They called me the boogeyman." He went silent, staring into the darkness. "They accepted me, even though I'm not the most talkative person."

"Really? I hadn't noticed."

He tugged on the end of her braid. "We went looking for a Taliban leader. He was high up the food chain, and we got word that he was hiding in a certain village. I was scouting the outskirts, while the others went in." He swallowed. He could almost feel the hot Afghan sun on his skin again. "It should have been a simple mission. Instead, I found a boy hiding in a field. His family was hiding close by, as well. I gave him some chocolate, and he told me that bad men had come to the village, and planted a bomb for the Americans." The air shuddered out of him. "I ran. They were walking into a trap. I couldn't raise them on the comms, and I knew the Taliban were jamming our signal."

Her hand tightened on his. "You ran back into a bomb zone."

"I had to try and save them."

She squeezed his hand. "Of course you did."

"I was getting close to the center of the village. It was eerily quiet. I saw the others on the other side the square, about to breach a building. I yelled. They looked up... And the bomb went off."

"I'm so sorry, Park."

"I came to with my ears ringing. I was hurt and couldn't move." He'd been hit by hot shrapnel and the pain had been bad. "There were just...body parts around me."

"Park." She pushed into his arms. "You have to remember them as they were. Not like that."

"I try." He held her tight. "Then the Taliban came. They were gloating about the kills, then they took me prisoner."

"I'm sorry."

"They kept me in a cell for twenty-two days."

She leaned into him.

He breathed in her scent to stay grounded. To stay in the present and not the past. "Twenty-two days of hell. I figured no one was coming. That I'd die there."

"But you survived."

"I almost didn't. They beat me daily."

She met his gaze. "Tell me."

"No. It..." These were the dark demons he'd been hiding from everyone. He hadn't told a soul.

"I'm strong enough to help you shoulder this. Let it out, Park. Don't let it haunt you."

A shudder ran through him. "They kept the lights on. I couldn't sleep. Sometimes, they hung me upside down when they beat the shit out of me. They cut me, burned me with acid. They'd put a plastic bag over my head and take me to the brink of death."

She didn't say a word, just held him tight. He focused on her warm body against his.

"I'd given up. I thought I'd die there. They wanted intel and I wouldn't give it to them. I was in agony, my wounds were infected...then my Ghost Ops team came."

He only had flashes of his rescue. He'd been too far out of it by then.

"Vander had rattled cages Stateside and got permission for my team to track me down."

"I'm guessing a man like Vander Norcross never leaves a man behind," she said.

"No, he doesn't. I woke up in a hospital in Germany and...I was broken. A nurse touched my arm, and I lost it. I knew I couldn't go back."

"You're not broken, Park. You know they didn't break you." She cupped his cheek. "They left their scars, sure, but I've seen your grit and determination. You're alive and breathing, and I'm guessing they aren't."

"No, my team took them out. But Leo and the others didn't come home."

She nodded. "I understand. I saw my marshals in the morgue in Fairbanks. But I try to remember them before. Calt was always making terrible dad jokes. Lopez loved football, tacos, and his grandkids." She smiled. "He'd always added that he'd never share exactly what order he'd rank them in."

Park cupped her face and kissed her. "Thank you."

"For what?"

"For listening. For understanding. For not asking a million questions."

"You just need time, Park. That's all. I guess Alaska's giving you that."

No, he was starting to think what he'd needed was Jenna Sheridan.

And that thought scared the hell out of him.

CHAPTER THIRTEEN

J enna woke and saw nylon, then blinked. She was in a tent.

She registered Park wrapped around her from behind, holding her tight. She smiled and enjoyed the moment. Enjoyed the feel of him, and the soft sound of his breathing. He was a man who the word soft rarely applied to anything about him.

It was time to admit that she was falling hard for this scarred, intense hero. She breathed deeply.

And it was too late, she couldn't stop it.

Her heart skipped a beat.

Maybe she didn't want to stop it.

Park's hand moved, sliding up under her T-shirt and cupped her breast. She sucked in a breath at the electric sensations.

"Good morning," she murmured.

"Usually, I don't care about anything when I wake up. I don't care about what day it is or what I'm going to do. I just wake up and get going." His voice was low and still raspy with sleep. "But waking up beside you changes everything."

His words made her chest hitch. He bit her neck, hitting a sensitive spot. With a gasp, she arched into him. He plucked at her nipple, taking his time to tease her. Her hand twisted in the sleeping bag covering them. Then his hand moved down her body, stroking her skin.

"*Park...*"

"I love the way you say my name." He bit her neck again, catching the tendon between his teeth.

Then his hand slid into her shorts, between her thighs, and stroked. She moved restlessly, desire coiling in her belly. With a growl, he shoved her shorts down her legs.

The hot need inside her built so fast and so high. It was always like this with him. He just had to touch her and she went up in flames.

He hitched her leg up and over his thigh, then she felt his hard cock brush her buttock. Anticipation skittered through her.

Then, he thrust into her from behind.

Jenna moaned. She was so full. So connected to him.

"*God*," he growled. "This is the best feeling ever, sliding inside of you."

Did he know how much those words got to her? How they made her feel?

Then he started thrusting.

In that moment, she didn't think about anything else. Couldn't think. It was just the two of them and all she could do was feel.

His thumb found her clit and his fingers stroked

where she was stretched around him. The speed of his thrusts picked up.

"Get there, Jenna."

She moaned. She felt her orgasm getting closer. All the sensations swirling inside her, centered on where this man was thrusting inside her.

"I'm close," she panted.

"Come for me. Now."

"*Yes!*" Suddenly, her climax hit in a wild, potent rush. "*Park.*"

He gripped her hip hard, and plunged inside her again and again. On his final thrust, he filled her deeply and groaned through his own release. His fingers bit into her skin.

They both lay there, panting hard as they fought to catch their breath.

"There are some perks to camping," she said.

Park's low laugh was music to her ears. That was laugh number two.

"I need to clean up," she murmured.

"I'll make coffee and breakfast. We need to pack up and get back on the trail."

She sat up. "You think he's close? Camping somewhere nearby?"

"I hope so."

Jenna hoped so too. She wanted Olson locked away where he couldn't hurt anyone else.

Soon, she and Park had changed, eaten, and packed up their gear.

It was warm today, with the sun shining overhead in a blue, cloudless sky. Jenna had worked up a sweat as they

ANNA HACKETT

hiked. The trees were sparse and the land here was flat. The mountains ahead were breathtaking.

"There's a public campground a few klicks away," Park said looking at the map.

"My guess is that he'd avoid people." Jenna scanned around. "He'd hide somewhere. In a place with a good vantage point and view. Somewhere where he can see us coming."

"Except the tops of all the mountains here have no trees. Doesn't leave many places to hide. He'll stay close." Park crouched. "He definitely came this way. Shoe print."

They kept moving, moving into an area with more trees. She breathed in the fresh, green, piney scent.

Suddenly, Park stopped. There was an intense look on his face.

She slowed her steps. "What is it?" She hadn't heard or seen anything. She looked into the trees, searching for what had set him off.

"I'm not sure," he said. "Something..."

Jenna took another step, her boot moving through a pile of leaf debris.

Click.

Suddenly, Parker's full weight hit her.

They flew through the air and hit the ground.

Boom.

Dirt and leaves rained over them.

"Oh God." Her heart thundered in her chest.

Park rolled them.

"Jenna, are you okay?" With a worried look on his face, he sat up, patting down her body.

142

"I'm okay." She tried to get her pulse to calm down.

"You sure?" He kept patting, a dark look in his eyes.

"Park." She cupped his scarred cheek. "I'm okay."

His gaze met hers and her chest locked. So dark, so tortured.

She leaned forward and kissed him.

He made a sound, then cupped her head, and took control of the kiss. It was hard, forceful. Jenna poured herself into it, wanting to comfort him.

When they broke apart, the sound of their raspy breathing filled her ears. He pressed his forehead to hers.

"That was a booby-trap," she said. "Like the ones at the Hoskins' place."

"Yeah. Olson mustn't be far away. This was a warning. It lets him know if anyone's close."

She stiffened. "He'll be coming."

"Or running from us." Park helped her up. "We'll have to move cautiously. There could be more booby-traps."

She nodded and looked at the trees. She registered a glint in the shadows under one large spruce.

Adrenaline hit her, and she rammed her shoulder into Park.

A bullet whizzed past and hit the tree trunk behind them.

WITHOUT HESITATION, Park pulled his handgun out and returned fire. He grabbed Jenna's arm, dragging her back behind a tree.

More gunfire filled the air.

They pressed together. She had a cool, focused look on her face. She wasn't afraid, she was pissed.

"We need to get over behind those rocks," he told her. "It'll give us better cover."

She studied the boulders and nodded. She pulled her own Glock out.

"I'll give you cover fire," he said.

"All right."

"On three. One. Two. *Three*." Park aimed into the trees and laid down fire. Jenna sprinted, moving quickly, then dove and rolled in behind the rocks. A second later, she popped up and started firing.

Park took off at a sprint. He zigzagged, and slid in beside her.

The shooting stopped.

"It's over, Olson," Jenna yelled. "The US Marshals Service is taking you in. You can keep running, but I'll keep coming."

"Good speech," a voice called back.

Park pressed his lips together. "That's him."

Olson fired again, and Park and Jenna ducked low. When there was a break in the hail of bullets, she raised her voice. "Stop wasting all our time. Just give yourself up. Make it easier for you."

"Let me think." There was a sarcastic edge to his voice. "No."

Olson fired on them again.

Park rose to his knees and fired back. Beside him, Jenna did the same.

They could get lucky and hit him.

They both pulled back into cover.

"You'll never catch me," Olson yelled, his voice echoing through the trees. "I'm not going back in."

"Because you like killing too much," Park yelled.

Olson was silent for a moment. "Just like you do. I should've figured they'd bring in someone from Ghost Ops to help find me. I remember you, Conroy. A quiet, boring do-gooder."

"I remember you too. An asshole."

They traded more gunshots.

"I don't think he likes you," Jenna said.

"I'm heartbroken."

"I saw you at the hunting cabin with the pretty marshal, Conroy. When I tried to blow her brains out."

Park tensed.

Jenna put a hand on his arm and shot him a warning look.

"And did you like my work with the older couple?" There was sick pleasure in the fucker's voice.

"Ah, but you were rushed," Jenna said. "You're just another two-bit killer, Olson. There's nothing special about you. You'll be in good company in prison."

Seconds ticked by. "You'll never catch me. Conroy, you're not as good as me. I heard you got captured. That you became the Taliban's plaything."

Park sucked in a breath, his fingers tightening on the butt of his gun.

"I'm going to make the pretty marshal my plaything," Olson continued. "Make you watch while I hurt her."

Park couldn't hold it in. He popped up and fired. He heard Olson's laughter somewhere in the trees.

With a curse, Park dropped back down and pressed his back to the rocks.

"Don't let him bait you," Jenna said.

He gave her a clipped nod. That was easier said than done. Especially when he threatened her.

No one was laying a hand on her.

No one was tying her up, keeping her captive, hurting her.

There were more shots, but Olson didn't say anything else.

Then the gunfire paused.

"Can we circle around to him?" she asked.

Park frowned. "There could be more booby-traps."

Another few shots came in their direction. Park leaned up and fired back.

They had to do something. They'd run out of ammo soon.

"Call Owen," he said. "We need back up."

Jenna nodded and pulled out her satellite phone.

Park sent a few more shots at Olson while Jenna urgently talked with Owen. The gunfire stopped again, and he frowned. He felt a whisper of unease. Why was Olson keeping them pinned down?

"Owen's on the way." She checked her weapon. "He'll be here with the state troopers in the helicopter soon."

"Something's not right," Park said.

"That spidey sense of yours is a little freaky."

"Vander's is worse." He rose into a crouch. "Stay here. I'll be back."

"Hell, no." She gripped his sleeve. "We go together."

"There's no point both of us leaving cover."

"Then I'll go."

"Absolutely not," he gritted out.

"I'm law enforcement. You're a civilian."

He made a sound. "Fine. We'll both go." Gunfire came their way again and he frowned.

"What is it?" she asked.

"It's the same amount of time between the shots."

Her brows drew together. "What?"

He rose but stayed low. "Follow me. Stay behind me."

Cautiously, he raced out of cover and ducked into the trees. Jenna stayed one step behind him.

Using the trees for cover, they approached Olson's location. There were more gunshots. Olson was still firing at the rocks where they'd been hiding.

They circled through the trees, and then Park cursed.

"What the hell?" Jenna said.

A handgun was set up on a stand. They moved in closer, and Park looked around, aiming his gun at the trees. There was no sign of Olson.

A second later, the gun fired again.

He'd rigged it to fire on a timed interval. Park cursed again.

"He set this up. To give himself a head start."

CHAPTER FOURTEEN

J enna followed behind Parker, stepping slowly and cautiously. They're both searching for any more booby-traps.

Inside, she was churning with anger. Olson was playing with them. Like this was a damn game.

She blew out a breath. But he was close. They could catch him. They *would* catch him.

She hated that they had to move at a snail's pace.

"We must be clear of any traps by now," she said.

"We don't know that." Park's tone was low and clipped.

"Park, we'll lose him. It's worth the risk."

His gaze locked on her face. "No. It's not."

She reached out and touched his arm. "We're clear. We need to run him down. Owen is still ten minutes out."

A muscle worked in his jaw. "*Dammit.*"

"Come on."

He nodded. "Avoid any piles of leaves, or any disturbed earth—"

"Got it."

Park broke into a fast lope, and Jenna rushed to keep up with him. They raced through the trees. A branch slapped at her arm, and she ignored it. In places, she and Park leaped over piles of leaves and dried branches.

Her chest was heaving a little when they finally reached a clearing. Park jerked to a halt.

"Stop."

She obeyed instantly. That spooky sixth sense of his... She was coming to depend on it.

He pointed.

She saw a mound of leaves. They looked dry and didn't look disturbed.

"Cover me," he said.

She pulled out her gun and lifted it. Turning in a half circle, she looked for any movement.

He cautiously moved into the clearing and knelt beside the leaves. He nudged them aside carefully.

She saw the explosive device.

Shit. Olson was still planting traps for them.

That's when she heard a repetitive *thump, thump, thump* in the sky. She smiled. "Owen is almost here."

Park carefully moved along the edge of the clearing, pausing to study the ground. "Olson went this way."

They moved into a jog. Park was on high alert, and she knew he was still keeping an eye out for more traps.

The trees thinned out and Jenna slowed. Olson could be waiting for them, and she didn't want to be caught with no cover. He'd pick them off easily.

"Any sign of him?" Park said.

She shook her head.

"I'm going to climb up a tree and take a look. Stay in cover." He gripped a branch, then pulled himself up in an easy display of strength. He climbed up the branches and disappeared from view.

She pulled out her satellite phone and hit the button. "Owen."

"We're close," Owen replied.

"We can hear the helo. We're at the bottom of the mountainside, where the trees thin out." She gave him the coordinates. "Olson's close."

"Have you got eyes on him?"

"Negative. Parker is in a tree, trying to spot him."

"Okay. We'll do a sweep of the area. See if we can get a bead on him."

"Acknowledged."

A moment later, Park dropped out of the tree. She almost jolted. He hadn't made a sound. There was a fierce frown on his face. "No sign of him."

Her heart dropped. "He's rabbited. I was sure he'd stay and fight."

Park's frown deepened. "I don't know. Something doesn't feel right."

Her chest tightened and she scanned the trees again. *Where the hell are you, Olson?*

A moment later, a blue-and-white helicopter came into view, sweeping in over the trees.

"They're looking for him," she said.

Parker nodded.

Crack.

In the air, the helicopter jolted and moved quickly to one side.

Crack.

"*Fuck.* Olson is shooting at the helicopter." Jenna grabbed the satellite phone. "Owen?"

"We're under fire. One pilot's been hit, so has the engine."

She watched as the helicopter swung west, the pilot clearly fighting for control.

"Olson's got a sniper rifle," Park said. "From the shots, I'd guess that he's north of our location."

"Owen, Park thinks Olson is to the north."

"The pilot's going to land," Owen said. "We'll move to the south."

She saw the helicopter start descending.

Her pulse raced and she dragged in a breath. At least they hadn't crashed.

"We need to check that they're okay." Park watched the helo until it disappeared from view. "Plus, we need more ammunition."

She nodded, frustration crashing into her. She wanted to track down her prey. Olson was getting away. She cursed.

Park grabbed her arm. "We'll get him."

———

WITH JENNA BY HIS SIDE, they raced to the area where the helicopter had landed. It was in a flat area with no trees.

Park felt the tension coming off her. She wanted to be

chasing Olson.

He glanced up at the mountains. They'd get him. They wouldn't give up.

A second later, they cleared the trees and he saw the helicopter. Several state troopers and Owen were milling around it.

"Owen!" Jenna jogged over and gripped the young marshal's hand. "Are you okay? Anyone injured?"

The younger man nodded. "We're all alive. One pilot got hit by shrapnel in the face and neck. The bullet shattered the glass." He nodded over to where a man in a white shirt sat on the ground. His shirt was sprinkled with blood and another state trooper was treating him.

The second pilot appeared, circling the helicopter. He was older, with a gruff face. He was checking the exterior of the aircraft.

He walked toward them.

"Chris, this is US Marshal Jenna Sheridan, and Parker Conroy," Owen said. "They're hunting the fugitive on the ground."

The pilot nodded.

"What's the verdict?" Owen asked.

"I can fix it," the man said.

"You're sure?" Jenna asked.

"I've been working on birds of all kinds my entire life. The bullet hit the engine, but the damage is minor. Oliver copped the worst of it." His gaze moved to his injured co-pilot.

"Okay, do whatever you need to do." Jenna looked back at Owen. "Olson is on the move, but he's close. This is our chance to stop him. If he gets away..."

"We'll never find him again." Owen frowned. "We need to wait for the helo to be fixed."

She shook her head. "If we wait, we'll lose him."

Owen looked at Parker.

Park inclined his head. "She's right. It's why Olson shot at the helo in the first place. He wanted our backup gone."

"Parker and I have this," she said. "Olson is running. He feels us closing in. He'll mess up and make mistakes. We can't give him a chance to regroup or he'll get away." Her face hardened. "And then he'll kill again. I'm *not* letting that happen."

Park reached out and touched her back. He hated seeing her upset, and knew that she still blamed herself for the Hoskins.

Owen didn't miss the move, his gaze narrowing on Park's hand.

"I'll have her back," Park said.

"Okay." The young marshal sighed and focused on Jenna. "I know you're too stubborn to listen anyway."

"I listen, I just don't always do what you think is right."

"Be careful. I didn't believe you when you first told me how dangerous Olson is. I do now. We'll get in the air and head your way soon as we can."

Jenna nodded. "Thanks, Owen."

The marshal turned to Parker. "Take care of her."

Park didn't need the order. "I will. Besides, she can take care of herself."

Jenna met his gaze and gave him half smile. "Let's move, Conroy."

Soon, they were running through the trees at a decent pace. Park didn't need to stop to find Owen's trail. He hadn't hidden it.

Park frowned. "He's heading north."

Jenna slowed and pulled out a map. She studied the terrain, then sucked in a breath. "Toward the public campground." She shoved the map back in her bag. "There could be people there."

Park bit back a curse. This time, it was Jenna who set the pace. She picked up speed, and Park made sure to stay two steps in front of her, keeping an eye out for booby-traps.

But it didn't seem that Olson was stopping to set them now. No, he was moving fast.

They were both sweaty and breathing hard when they burst into the campground.

It wasn't fancy, but it had a breathtaking view of the mountains. There were some wooden picnic tables, a water pump, and in the distance, some toilets.

There was one large, red tent set up. Two fold-up chairs sat beside it. The front entrance of it was unzipped and flapping in the breeze.

"No." Jenna took off at a run toward the tent.

"*Jenna.*" He followed, pulling his weapon.

She slowed down and dragged in a breath. She pulled her own gun from its holster.

"You good?" he murmured.

She nodded but she had a dark look in her eyes. He knew she was afraid of what they'd find inside.

Then she nudged the flap open wide. With her gun

aimed, she entered the tent. Park moved right in behind her.

A second later, she shoved the gun away and released a breath. "US Marshals. You're safe now."

Park sidestepped Jenna and saw the older couple tied up on the ground in the tent. The man had blood running down the side of his head. It looked like he'd been hit with the butt of a gun. The woman's dark hair was disheveled, her eyes wide. Their mouths were taped up.

Jenna untied the woman, while Park freed the man. He ripped the tape off the man's mouth.

"Oh, thank the Lord," the woman said shakily.

"You're safe now," Jenna said. "I'm US Marshal Jenna Sheridan. What are your names?"

"Phil and Brenda Cochran," the man said.

"Okay, Phil and Brenda." Jenna's voice was low and soothing. "Don't worry. We're going to take care of you. Can you tell me who did this?"

"A man." Phil swallowed. "Um, he was tall, fit, had brown hair."

"Red," Brenda added, her voice thin and still shaky. "His hair was reddish-brown."

"He's a fugitive that we're tracking." Park checked the man's head. "Looks like you need some stitches, Phil."

"He was so...frightening," Brenda said. "His eyes were cold." She shivered.

The pair were lucky to be alive.

"What did he want?" Jenna asked.

Phil swallowed. "He took some food, my hunting knife, and our vehicle."

Jenna cursed. "What model car? What color? What's your number plate?"

"It's a Toyota 4Runner. Blue." Phil rattled off his plate.

Jenna pulled out the phone. "I need to relay the information to Owen."

"Go," Park said.

She stepped outside and he heard the murmur of her voice.

"Marshal Sheridan is going to call in help," Park told the couple. "You're safe now."

Brenda grabbed Park's hand. For the first time in ages, he didn't yank his hand back.

"You'll capture him? You'll make sure he doesn't hurt anyone else?"

"Yes, ma'am. That's exactly what we're going to do."

"You look like a man who keeps your promises."

Park nodded.

There was a rustle of nylon and Jenna stepped back inside. "They finished repairs and the helicopter is coming this way. The state troopers have the details for the 4Runner and have put out a BOLO alert."

Park met her gaze. "Good. Let's chase his ass down."

CHAPTER FIFTEEN

E ven with the headset on, the rhythmic *thump* of the helicopter rotors echoed in her ears.

Jenna scanned the road below for Olson and the blue Toyota.

Nothing.

Where the hell was he? There weren't loads of roads around this area of Alaska. Frustration cut through her. He could be hiding somewhere. He could have hidden the SUV and was laying low.

She looked over at Owen and touched her headset. "Any word from the police or state troopers on the ground? Has anyone spotted Olson's vehicle?"

Owen shook his head.

Dammit. She ground her teeth together.

Fingers touched hers. Park was sitting still and quiet beside her, his eyes closed.

"How can you be so calm?" she asked.

His eyes opened and he raised a brow. "Me looking out the window won't help find him. You have people searching for him. It's best I conserve my energy for when we do find him."

She blew out a breath. "I can't rest."

"Just takes practice. I used to be able to take a nap in the middle of a warzone when needed."

"I think he's holed up," she said. "He's found a barn or some dense trees..."

Park shook his head.

She swiveled to face him. "Why not?"

"It's too hot. He knows you'll keep hunting him. His face is everywhere, and he wants out of Alaska."

She chewed on her lip and looked down at the road again. "Where will he go? Anchorage?"

Park shook his head. "Anchorage is too busy. He wouldn't be able to get through the airport."

She nodded slowly. "So, a small airport. Or—"

"A boat," Park said. "There are lots of commercial fishing towns along the coast."

"And plenty of boats willing to take on an able-bodied man who's fit, no questions asked." She waved a hand. "Owen, I need a map. We need to see the main fishing towns between Drifter Lake and the coast."

A moment later, Owen unfolded a map. With a marker, he started circling the towns along the coastline.

There were more than she'd hoped.

Park pressed a hand to her knee and squeezed. "We're going to get him."

They would. They wouldn't stop until they did. And she knew Park—with his steady presence and support—would be with her all the way.

But what if Olson killed again before they did? He

was on the run, but the urge could get too much for him to ignore.

No. There would be no more death.

The helicopter continued to follow the main road from Drifter Lake heading toward the coast. There was no sign of Olson.

They stopped to refuel, and every second felt like a damn week. Once they were back in the air, Jenna prayed that they'd find him.

Owen tapped her shoulder, excitement on his face.

"A man had his Subaru Outback stolen near Copperville. It's on the road to the coast. Troopers found the 4Runner stashed nearby."

She snatched the map and ran her finger along until she found Copperville. "He switched cars. Get the troopers looking for the Subaru."

"I can do one better than that." Owen smiled. "The Outback was spotted in Valdez."

Her heart leaped into her throat. She looked at the map. Valdez was one of the fishing towns they'd circled.

"Valdez is a fishing port." Owen looked at his phone. "Both commercial and sport fishing. Plus, freight moves through the port into Alaska. The town is located on a deep fjord in the Prince William Sound, and surrounded by mountains and glaciers." He flicked the screen. "The town sits at the southern end of the Trans-Alaska Oil Pipeline. There's a dedicated oil terminal across the bay from the town where the oil is loaded onto ships."

"This is where the *Exxon Valdez* disaster happened, right?" Park said.

Owen lifted his chin. "The ship was loaded in

Valdez. It ran aground and spilled its cargo in Prince William Sound, and although hundreds of miles of coastline was affected, Valdez itself wasn't."

"Tell the pilot to get us there fast." Jenna looked up at Park. "We're closing in. We are not letting him get away."

"Marshal Sheridan, I'd never bet against you." His lips quirked. "I suspect you always get your man."

"I do."

But the hunt for Olson aside, she knew the man she really wanted was this one. This loner who held everything in. He was good and honorable, and lived with the scars of the things he'd seen and done. And had done to him.

She clenched her hands together and looked out the helicopter window. She barely saw the mountains below. She wondered if this time she'd get her man.

Now is not the time, Jenna. She pulled in a steadying breath.

Once Olson was in custody, then she'd turn her formidable skills onto Parker Conroy.

Soon the coastline came into view. Valdez was located up a fjord, the blue water ringed by wild mountains. It was beautiful.

"We're coming into land," Owen said.

Jenna spotted the airport. It was just outside the town.

"The troopers are meeting us with vehicles," Owen said.

It wasn't long before Jenna was leaping off the helicopter and striding toward one of the black SUVs waiting for them.

"Owen, I need you to stay here and coordinate with the state troopers."

He jerked to a halt. "I want to help chase down Olson."

"I know. I need you to get a roadblock set up on the highway out of Valdez. And talk to the harbormaster, and stop any boats leaving."

He pressed a hand to the back of his neck.

"I know you want to be in the action, but this is important."

He nodded. "I'm on it."

She slid into the driver's seat, and Park climbed into the passenger seat beside her.

"The Subaru was spotted parked downtown," Owen said. "Not far from the boat harbor."

She nodded and studied the map of Valdez. "This ends today."

Her fellow marshal nodded. "Be careful. Both of you."

Jenna started the engine and pulled out.

Soon, they drove into the town, passing under a large arch that proclaimed, *Valdez, Alaska*. The town wasn't big, with wide streets and buildings spaced out. If she hadn't been so focused on finding Olson, she would have taken more time to admire the stunning mountains that ringed the water.

She drove past the harbor, noting all the docks filled with boat slips. Hundreds of boats bobbed on the water. She turned into the next street, noting some restaurants and other businesses. She parked, and they climbed out.

"We don't want to stick out." Park took her hand.

ANNA HACKETT

Jenna curled her fingers around his. He kept his pace slow and easy, and she guessed at a glance they looked like a tourist couple out for a stroll.

There were more people on the sidewalk than she'd anticipated.

"They come for the fishing," Park murmured. "And the hiking and glaciers."

She carefully searched around. There was no sign of Olson. Two men—fishermen, she guessed—stumbled out of a bar. One was singing at the top of his lungs, while the other wavered on his feet. They were clearly drunk. She glanced up at the sign above—*The Taphouse*.

"Maybe Olson wanted a drink?" she suggested.

Park held the door of The Taphouse open for her, and they stepped inside.

This place wasn't fancy, but it had a decent crowd. She saw a server setting plates topped with huge crab legs down on a table. At the bar, several men were sipping beers with Valdez Brewing written on the glasses.

She and Park found a high table, and she leaned against it, looking around the bar discreetly.

"I'll buy us some drinks, to help us blend in." Park headed for the bar.

Jenna saw tourists, fishermen that she guessed came from the commercial boats, and a few locals. She hadn't really expected to find Olson here, but a bar was his favorite hunting ground.

The pressure was on him. Maybe the urge to kill would get the better of him.

Park returned with two beers, and she made herself take a sip.

162

"Did you see him?" she asked.

Park shook his head. "The bartender hasn't seen him either."

At a table nearby, some of the fishermen got rowdy, and started singing. A female server hurried past, balancing a tray full of drinks. Across the bar, there was a man with a black knit hat on his head. He turned and his gaze locked with hers.

Olson.

Her pulse kicked into gear. "Park."

He lifted his head and spotted Olson.

More people rose and joined in the singing. They blocked Jenna's view of her quarry.

"Dammit." She shot to her feet and pushed through the crowd.

Then she spotted Olson again. He turned to a fisherman and swung his fist. He punched the man right in the face.

That was all it took.

With a roar, the fisherman swung, but instead of hitting Olson, he hit another man.

"What the fuck?" the recipient of the punch bellowed.

A brawl broke out.

Jenna couldn't get through. Across the chaos, Olson smiled at her, then slipped out the back door.

PARK SHOULDERED out of The Taphouse.

They were only seconds behind Olson, but that was

all he needed.

As they chased after Olson into a back alley behind the bar, he noticed a nearby dumpster, a parked truck, and a couple of shipping containers he guessed were for storage. "Dammit, I don't see him." Jenna put her hands on her hips as she looked around.

Park sensed something. "That way." He turned left and took off at a run. His entire focus narrowed in on chasing Olson.

It ended here. *Today*.

Olson had put Ghost Ops to shame, and Park wouldn't let it stand. Most of all, he wanted Jenna safe.

Jenna kept pace with him. They ran out of the alley and onto the street. There were several tourists walking on the sidewalk. Across the street was an empty lot with some RVs parked in it. A double-story building that housed several shops lay just beyond that. Cheery, colorful flower boxes decorated the front of it.

Park slowed down, making himself really look at everyone walking nearby. There was a laughing couple, a family with several teenagers who were all hunched over their cellphones, some older couples he guessed were vacationing together. Then he spotted a man near the corner, moving fast.

He wore a black, knit hat.

"There." Park skirted some people and broke into a run.

Olson glanced back and spotted them. He ripped the hat off his head, then shoved a nearby woman. With a cry, she tripped over and hit the concrete.

Park leaped over her.

"Help her," Jenna yelled at someone.

Olson turned a corner and Park followed. He saw Olson dart across the street. As Park ran out, a car screeched to a halt, narrowly missing him.

Fuck.

As a horn blared, Park pressed one palm to the hood, slid across it, and kept going.

Ahead, Olson disappeared down the next street.

Park rounded the corner, blood pumping. A long, low building housing a hotel was on one side. The Harbor Inn. On the other were some trailer homes. There was no sign of Olson. No sign of anyone.

"Fuck," he muttered.

Jenna caught up with him. "Where did he go?"

"I don't know." They walked down the sidewalk, searching.

"There!" Jenna pointed up.

There was a flash of movement and Parker saw Olson on the roof of the inn. The man was running along it and moving quickly.

Park took off. Ahead, he spotted a dumpster beside the end of the building and leaped on top of it. He jumped up, caught the edge of the roof, then hauled himself up.

He looked back down at Jenna.

"Go!" she yelled. "Get him and I'll follow."

Park straightened. His gaze locked on Olson and he set off after the man. He carefully navigated the roof. Ahead, Olson reached the edge of the building and leaped across the small gap to the next building.

He was gaining on Olson. The man glanced back and saw him coming.

That's right. I'm coming for you.

Park pumped his arms and closed the distance. He leaped across another gap.

Olson reached the end of the second building. The next building was too far away for him to jump to. He stopped, but Parker didn't. He picked up speed and hit Olson.

They flew off the edge of the building. The ground below raced up at them.

Park braced, then shoved Olson away from him. He landed and rolled, ignoring the aches and pains that rattled through him. He'd had worse landings.

Olson landed badly. He was flat on his stomach, breathing hard, his face twisted. Unsteadily, he pushed to his feet.

They were standing between a brick building and a parked truck. No one could see them from the street.

Parker pulled out his gun and advanced on him. "It's over, Olson."

Olson straightened, then yanked a knife off his belt. "A good Ghost Ops soldier never gives up."

"You are *not* Ghost Ops. You never were."

Olson smiled. "You hate knowing that I'm better than you." He threw the knife, the move fast and sure.

The knife hit Park's gun, nicking his hand. The gun fell from his fingers.

Quickly, he spun, blocking Olson's kick. Olson came at Park again and they traded several hard, brutal blows.

Olson pulled back. Now, he pulled out a second

knife. This one was a tactical knife—the same one they'd carried in Ghost Ops. It was designed to kill.

They circled each other.

"You shouldn't have agreed to hunt a brother," Olson said.

"You're not my brother. You're a murderer."

Olson lunged and swung the knife.

Park barely leaped back in time. The guy was fast.

Olson smiled. "I think I'll enjoy gutting you. Then, I'll find your marshal."

Park ground his teeth together until his jaw hurt. The thought of Olson anywhere near Jenna made him see red.

"You don't like that, do you?" Olson drawled.

"I don't like you at all."

They circled in the opposite direction, then Olson attacked.

Park blocked the knife and punched the man in the side. His grunt was music to Park's ears. But Olson whirled and rammed his elbow into Park's chest. The fight turned vicious. Their arms moved fast, as they both blocked and dodged hits. Park got some blows in, but so did Olson.

He forced himself to ignore the pain. Win the fight, take Olson down, that was all that mattered.

"Parker!" Jenna's shout echoed off the brick wall of the nearby building.

The minute distraction was all Olson needed. There was a flash of the knife, and Park felt a hot sting on his arm.

With a hiss, he pulled back.

Olson grinned.

Park refocused. When Olson swung again, he timed it right and grabbed the man's arm and twisted.

Olson grunted, then Park rammed him head first into the wall.

"Kyle Olson, you're under arrest." Jenna stepped into view, her gun aimed at Olson. "Drop the knife."

Park squeezed Olson's arm, and the knife dropped to the ground.

All of a sudden, Olson whipped his free hand up.

"He has another knife!" Jenna yelled.

Dammit, how many blades was the guy carrying? Park jerked to the side, but he wasn't quick enough.

The knife stabbed into his side. Pain sizzled through him, and he heard Jenna cry out.

He wrenched away from Olson. The man still clutched the knife in his hand and it was covered in blood.

Park tried to stay upright, but a wave of dizziness hit. He fell to the ground. *Dammit to hell.*

Jenna fired, and Olson turned and pulled out his own gun.

"Jenna, get into cover," Park yelled.

She ignored him.

He had to get up. He had to help Jenna. Pain drilled through his hip and side, and he gritted his teeth. He got to his knees.

Olson smiled. "Oh, yes, the pretty marshal and I are going to have so much fun."

Fuck. Helplessness hit him, squeezing his insides. For a second, he felt like he was back running through that village. Knowing he'd be too late to save his fellow soldiers.

No. This was Jenna. Failure wasn't an option.

Park got one foot under him.

Clunk.

Something metallic rolled into view.

Frowning, Olson turned.

Parker knew exactly what it was. He closed his eyes and turned his head away.

The flash bang went off with a blinding flash of light and an ear-splitting noise. In the chaos, he heard Jenna scream his name.

CHAPTER SIXTEEN

J enna shook her head. She was bent over, her ears were ringing and her vision was blurry.

She couldn't see Olson.

Two dark shapes dropped from the roof of the nearby building.

What the hell? Did Olson have accomplices? Were they here to help him escape?

She straightened, using the wall to hold herself up. She lifted her arm and tried to aim her gun. "Freeze. US Marshals."

"Don't worry, we're on your side," a deep voice said.

Jenna sucked in a breath and blinked at the men. "Vander?"

"Olson's running," the other male said.

"Go after him," Vander said. "I've got Park and Jenna."

The other man took off running down the alley.

Park.

Her vision hadn't cleared entirely, but she saw him

lying on the ground and stumbled toward him. He had a hand pressed to his side. Blood oozed between his fingers.

"Park!" She dropped to her knees.

"Jenna, are you okay?" he asked. "A flash bang leaves you disoriented. Just breathe."

"I'm fine. Olson stabbed you." She slid her gun away and touched his side. There was so much blood.

"Your warning meant that he didn't hit anything vital."

"Let me see." She lifted his hand and her breath hitched. Iciness pooled in her belly. It looked bad. She pushed her palm down hard on the injury and he grunted. "We need to stop the bleeding."

It was clear that Olson had been aiming to kill. Just a few millimeters in the other direction and...

Her throat tightened, a storm of emotions raging inside her.

She couldn't lose Park.

Vander crouched on the other side of Park.

"Where did you come from?" Park said.

"I was in the neighborhood."

"Always had uncanny timing."

"You do too." Vander held up Park's HK. "Think this belongs to you."

"Thanks."

Vander slid a sleek backpack off his shoulders and pulled out a small first aid kit. A moment later, he pressed a bandage to Park's wound. He met Jenna's gaze. "Olson is our mess to help clean up. I called some friends, and we came as fast as we could. I found out that you'd tracked Olson here to Valdez."

ANNA HACKETT

She was sure Vander had all kinds of contacts in law enforcement, and probably in shadier circles as well. He liked to keep his finger on the pulse of everything.

Footsteps echoed on the pavement and a tall, muscular man appeared. He wore a flannel shirt and had a strong jaw and a steady gaze.

"Olson got away." A muscle ticked in his jaw. "He's slippery."

"Hi, Boone," Park said through gritted teeth.

"Hey, Park. You doing okay?"

"He needs stitches," Vander said. "Shep can do it. He's surprisingly neat at it."

"Except he has a rotten bedside manner," Boone said with a smile.

"Shep's here too?" Park said.

"Yes, and so is Ren," Vander added. "Sawyer would've come as well, but he's out of the country with Hollis. Boone, this is US Marshal Jenna Sheridan."

The man in the flannel nodded at her. "Bad circumstances, but nice to meet you."

"You too."

"We've got a room at a nearby hotel." Vander straightened. "Let's get Park back there before he bleeds to death."

Both men helped Park up, and kept him between them with his arms draped over their shoulders. Park's shirt was soaked with blood and Jenna bit her lip.

"He needs a hospital."

"No, I don't," Park bit out. He met her gaze. "No hospitals."

Her heart squeezed.

"We can treat him, Jenna, I promise," Vander said.

Together, their small group made it out onto the street. They walked toward a large black Suburban. Vander helped Park into the backseat while Boone circled around and got behind the wheel.

Jenna slid in beside Park. "Okay?"

"I will be." He took her hand.

His face was paler than usual, but he had the same tough glint in his eye.

"Promise?"

His lips quirked. "I promise. Can't get rid of me that easily."

That was her problem. She didn't want to get rid of him at all.

She was falling hard and fast for this former soldier.

Soon, Boone pulled up in front of a simple building painted a pale gray with a white trim. It was called the Glacier Hotel. Boone parked in front of one of the rooms. The front door opened, and a tall man walked out.

A second later, the back door of the Suburban opened.

"Park, you didn't let that asshole get the better of you, did you?" the newcomer said.

Jenna blinked. The guy was handsome. He had tousled, black hair, a chiseled face, and warm, brown eyes.

"It was just a love tap, Ren," Park said. "Good to see you."

Ren and Boone helped Park toward the door of a nearby room. A big, scowling man stood in the doorway, his broad shoulders filling the space.

"Shep, Ren, this is Jenna," Vander said. "She's with the US Marshals."

"Hi." Her gaze narrowed on Shep. "Wait, aren't you the guy who rescued the president's daughter when she was taken hostage in the jungle?"

"Yeah." Shep's voice was a deep rumble.

"He also fell in love with her," Ren added. "And they're going to get married."

Shep shot his friend a grumpy look.

Something told Jenna that grumpy was Shep's default. But right now, she didn't have time to chitchat. She was worried about Parker and the amount of blood he was losing. "Can you get Park into the bathroom. I'll stitch him up."

"You sure?" Vander asked.

"I'm sure."

They walked through the room that had two queen beds, a desk, and a TV. The bathroom wasn't fancy, with a shower above the tub and a slightly yellowing vanity and sink.

"Give us a shout if you need us," Ren said.

She helped Park take his shirt off, then sit on the closed toilet seat. He did a bad job of hiding his wince.

She opened Vander's first aid kit and briskly started cleaning the blood off his skin. The cut was nasty. He could've died. Her hand shook. "You're going to have another scar."

"Hey." He cupped her face with one big hand. "I'm okay."

"You could have bled out..."

"But I didn't. I'm pretty tough." He leaned forward and pressed his lips to hers.

She gripped his arm. "You're not invincible, Parker."

"Don't need to be when I have you guarding my back." He kissed her again.

With a small moan, she opened for him. She poured all her fear and worry into the kiss.

There was a faint sound and Vander walked in. "Oh. Sorry." He backed out of the bathroom with a half smile on his face.

"I don't like you getting hurt," she said. "Don't let it happen again."

He smiled. "I'll do my best."

She gave him some painkillers, then washed all the blood off her hands. Next, she painstakingly stitched up the cut. He didn't make a sound.

"So, your friends are here," she said.

"They want to stop Olson."

"And they want to help you."

"Yeah. But I'm not sure I need their help, not when I have you."

Her insides turned to warm mush. She finished the stitches and pressed a bandage over the wound. "Don't forget it. And whatever happens next, you're not to get hurt again. Understand?"

"Yes, ma'am."

She pressed her forehead to his. "I need to call Owen, and then I need to get back out there and find Olson."

Park grabbed her hand. "*We* need to get back out there."

She knew she had zero chance of getting him to stay here and rest. She nodded. "Yes, we're a team."

"YOU SHOULD BE IN BED. Or in a hospital."

Park glanced over at Jenna's surly tone.

"I'm okay." They were outside, walking down one of Valdez's streets again.

"I just stitched you up and mopped up the blood. So, I know that you're not okay."

There was a low chuckle behind them. Park knew it was Boone. Asshole. He was well aware that all his friends were watching them with amusement.

Park grabbed her hand. "Jenna, I'm fi—"

She glared at him.

"I'll heal. And I can finish this mission. I have you to protect me."

"Okay, listen up," Vander said.

They all turned.

"Kyle Olson is close. The only road out of the town is closed. We're taking him down. We'll split up in pairs. Boone and I will head that way." Vander pointed. "Ren and Shep will go back toward the bars. Park and Jenna will move toward the waterfront and harbor."

They all nodded.

"Olson is here," Vander said. "We're not letting him get away."

"I've checked in with my partner Deputy Marshal Owen Briggs. He's at the roadblock with the state troopers. He'll let us know if they catch Olson trying to get out of Valdez."

Park's mouth flattened. The net was tightening. Olson couldn't escape them now.

But he wouldn't go down without a hell of a fight.

"Let's find this fucker," Shep growled.

With a nod, they all broke apart. Park ignored the pull in his side. The cut hurt, but the painkillers had taken the edge off. He'd refused to take anything too strong. He didn't want to dull his senses.

He needed to focus on Olson.

And he didn't want Jenna to worry.

"He could've found somewhere to hide," Jenna said.

"No. He was at that bar to find a victim. He's not going to hide. He's under pressure, and he needs to kill to keep himself balanced."

Her face turned pinched. "We need to stop him before that happens."

They headed down the sidewalk and he took her hand.

"Try and look more like a woman on vacation and less like a badass marshal hunting down a fugitive."

She huffed, trying to relax.

He shook his head. "Nope, you still look like a marshal."

"Look, there's another bar." It was across from the harbor. "The Singing Mermaid." There was a carved wooden mermaid sitting near the front door.

They slowed down as they approached. Some people were sitting at tables outside, taking in the view of the mountains across the bay.

"See anything?" she asked.

"No."

"Sense anything with those spidey senses?"

He gave her ass a light swat. "Smart ass."

"How's the cut?"

"Stop thinking about it."

"I can't. He tried to kill you."

"He tried to kill you, too."

She squeezed his fingers. "Let's get this done, and stay alive while we do it."

They peered through the windows of the Singing Mermaid, but she didn't see Olson inside. They continued down the street.

There were so many boats bobbing in the harbor, docked at several slips. A cool breeze blew in, playfully tugging at Jenna's hair, and bringing the scent of fish. He saw a carved wooden sign that said *The Fishing is Great in Valdez, Alaska.* Several fish that looked like salmon hung off the sign, and people were taking photos.

"Leave my man alone, asshole!"

The female screech came from around the corner.

Jenna and Park shared a look, then picked up speed. They ran around the corner and saw another bar. This one wasn't as nice as the others they'd seen.

Two men were scuffling outside. A woman in a short skirt was hovering nearby and yelling. The taller man shoved the shorter guy away.

That's when Park got a clear view of the taller man's face.

It was Olson.

Park and Jenna broke into a run.

Olson looked over his shoulder and saw them coming. He shoved the man into the woman, and the pair crashed to the ground in a tangle. Olson took off.

Jenna followed, moving fast. Park ignored the pain in his side, blocking it out, and followed her.

Olson dashed across the street and headed for the harbor. He sprinted down the boardwalk, past a group of men cleaning fish, and down one of the entrances onto the docks.

Park and Jenna ran out onto the main dock. Olson was nowhere in sight. Several docks ran off it like arms.

"He can't have gone far," Jenna said. "You take that one—" she pointed at the closest dock "—and I'll go this way."

Split up? Hell, no. "We should stay together."

"We could lose him." Her face was set in hard lines. "Go, Park. He could circle back up that other dock or steal a boat."

Damn, he had to trust her. His jaw clenched, but he nodded.

He hadn't known her long, but there was no one he trusted more than Jenna.

As she moved down the dock to the left, he moved to the one on the right. He pulled out his gun. There were boats lined up on either side. These were all working fishing boats, and the scent of rotting fish was ripe.

He glanced through the boats to his left, catching a glimpse of Jenna on the neighboring dock, her gun in hand.

He focused back on his dock and the boats around him.

Where are you, Olson?

He peered in the back of several boats. No one was around. He walked on and looked in the back of the next boat.

There was no sound, just a hard hit to the center of his back.

Park stumbled, and caught his balance before he fell in the water. His gun flew from his hand and landed in the water with a *plop*. *Shit*. He spun.

Just in time to block Olson's kick.

The man didn't talk or taunt this time. He attacked—hard and brutal.

They traded blows. They grabbed at each other, shoving hard. Park gritted his teeth and put all his strength into it. Olson took a step back, then he yanked an arm free, and rammed his fist into Park's injured side.

With a grunt, he fought to hold on. His vision wavered. The pain was horrible.

Olson smiled. "I'm going to have fun with her."

He shoved Park hard. With a curse, Park hit the wooden dock, pain rolling through him. He fought back the urge to vomit.

He was back in that cell, hanging upside down, nothing but a mass of pain.

Not now. He pushed the old memories back. He couldn't pass out. Jenna needed him.

A second later, Olson tossed some heavy fishing nets on top of him, pinning him down.

"Jenna!" Park roared a warning. "He's here!"

Olson's running footsteps thudded on the dock as he sprinted away.

Park fought the nets and the pain, trying to get free. Finally, he shoved the heavy nets off his legs and pushed to his feet. Holding his side, he hobbled down the dock.

"Park!"

He looked up and saw Vander and the others running toward him.

"Olson's here." *Where was Jenna?* He scanned the docks and didn't see her. "Jenna!"

Then he saw something at the end of the dock she'd been searching. He picked up speed and moved into a jog.

He stopped at the end of the dock. *No.*

It was her gun.

Vander and the others arrived. Park snatched up her Glock, his chest feeling like it was filled with concrete.

He scanned around the harbor. "Olson has Jenna."

There was a roar of an engine. Park spun and saw a boat speeding away from the dock.

"Hey!" a man yelled from nearby. "Someone stole my boat."

Olson had Jenna and he was making a run for it.

"We have to stop him," Park growled. "Now!"

Hold on, Jenna. I'm coming for you.

CHAPTER SEVENTEEN

P ark couldn't breathe. He couldn't focus.

"Olson has Jenna. They're on that boat."

Vander cursed. "We need a boat."

"I'm on it," Ren said, jogging off toward the harbor-master's office.

It would take too long. Olson would hurt Jenna, or worse. Park turned and ran down the dock.

"Park!" Vander bellowed.

"I'm going to get my woman back." Park pulled his phone out and stabbed at the button. He held it to his ear.

"Deputy Marshal Briggs."

"Owen. Olson's got Jenna. He stole a boat."

"*Fuck*," Owen said.

"We have to get to her. We need the helo."

"I'll get it. Where are you?"

"At the harbor. Pick me up at the waterfront."

"Be ready. I'm on my way."

The minutes ticked by, and it felt like a fucking eter-nity. Then, Park heard the familiar *thump* of rotor blades.

He looked up and the blue-and-white State Trooper helicopter came into view. It swept in low over the town.

The wind battered him as it lowered toward the street in front of him. The downdraft flattened his shirt to his body.

It was still hovering several feet above the ground when Owen slid the side door open. Park ran and leaped aboard.

"Go," he said.

As he sat in a seat, the tail of the helicopter lifted, and the pilot flew them out over the harbor. The boats below looked like toys.

A boat was maneuvering out of the harbor. That would be Vander and the guys.

"Olson's got Jenna on a boat," Owen said, his face grim.

Park nodded and looked out the side window. Soon, they were over the open water of the bay, and he saw the trail in the water. In the distance, he saw Olson's boat.

Hold on, Jenna. Hold the fuck on.

"Jenna's tough," Owen said. "The toughest person I know."

Park nodded. "I know." His jaw was tight and he fought his fear down.

He hadn't wanted to feel again. After the torture, after he'd seen those good soldiers die, he hadn't wanted to feel anything.

His motto had been stay alone. Stay numb.

Jenna had blown all that to pieces.

He couldn't live without her.

"I love her. Fuck."

Owen's eyes went wide.

"Forget I said that," Park said.

"Ah, that would be impossible." Owen dragged in a breath. "Must have been a hell of a hike in the wilderness."

Park shot the man a look.

"I've known her almost a year. She deserves someone who recognizes her strength and skills. Who loves and respects her for it."

"She's the strongest, most amazing woman I've ever met." Park raked a hand over his head. "Hell, I didn't want to fall in love. She did this to me."

A small smile crossed Owen's face. "Well, I know you're strong enough to meet her toe to toe. And smart enough to not get in her way while she's doing her job."

Park grunted.

"Use what you feel to fuel you. To bring her back."

Park nodded.

The helicopter gained on the boat.

"Here," Owen said, holding out a handgun.

Park took it, checked it, then tucked it into his holster. "Thanks. Mine's in the bottom of the harbor." Then, he pulled in some calming breaths.

He cleared his mind the best he could. He had to save Jenna.

He had to put Olson down, once and for all.

They were his mission objectives. And he was a man who always finished his mission.

They got close enough to see the deck of the boat. He spotted Jenna with her hands tied in front of her, and tied to a pole that he guessed would hold fishing nets. There were stacks of nets and ropes on the flat deck at the back of the boat.

Owen was at the boat controls, standing under a small roof.

Park saw Jenna yelling something at Olson, then the man turned and slapped her.

Park stiffened. The man had signed his death warrant.

"Get us as close as you can," Park yelled at the pilot.

The man nodded.

Olson looked up at them and pulled a gun from his waistband. He aimed upward and fired at the helicopter. They jerked to the side, and Park almost lost his balance.

"Shit." Owen gripped one of the seats.

"Closer," Park barked.

The pilot looked back. "If he hits something vital, we'll all—"

"*Closer*," Park repeated.

He was pretty sure the pilot cursed, but the man swung in over the boat. Park slid the door open.

"Parker, what the hell have you got planned?" Owen said.

Park ignored the marshal. His focus was on the boat below. Suddenly, he saw Jenna break free of the pole and attack Olson.

The man swung a fist at her.

No.

Park braced himself in the open doorway of the helicopter.

Then, he leaped out.

OLSON'S FIST hit her cheek.

Pain exploded across her face.

Jenna was free of the pole, but her wrists were still bound. The roar of the boat engine and the helicopter dominated everything.

She looked up and saw Park in the helicopter. He'd come for her. He'd never let her down.

Energy poured into her. This ended here.

She kicked Olson. He stumbled back into the helm. She rammed into him again.

"I'm going to kill you," he spat. "I'll rape you until you scream, then I'll stab you until you cry."

"I'm not afraid of you, Olson." She drove an elbow into his face. She felt his nose break.

He bellowed, then his next blow hit her cheek. Her ears rang and she stumbled back.

Shit, that hurt like hell. She felt her face swelling.

He laughed loudly over the sound of the helicopter, and it was harsh and ugly. He took a step toward her, battling the pitch of the boat.

Then she saw movement out of the corner of her eye and looked up.

Her heart lodged in her throat.

Parker leaped from the helicopter.

Oh, God.

A second later, he hit the deck and rolled. Then he was up on his feet.

"You don't fucking touch her." Without pause, he attacked Olson.

The pair crossed the deck, trading blows. They fought hard—vicious kicks, violent punches. Then they slammed into each other, straining. It almost looked like they weren't doing anything, but she knew they were using all their strength and energy to grapple.

They broke apart and Park landed a punch to Olson's head. He jerked to the side and spat blood on the deck.

Then, he charged, his face twisted. Park dodged, but Olson caught him and hammered two hard punches into his gut.

Park winced and grabbed him, chopping a hard hit into his back.

Jenna fought her bindings. She had to get free and help him.

She saw Park ram a knee up into Olson's stomach, then step back. He pulled out a handgun. Olson kicked his leg up and caught the gun. It flew through the air and hit the railing. She gasped. For a second, she was sure it would tip over the edge and into the water.

Instead, it hit the deck and slid out of view.

"You have nowhere to go, Olson," Park gritted out.

"I'm smarter and better than all of you." Olson smirked. "I'll get away. I always do."

Park shook his head. "See that boat incoming."

Jenna looked to the side and saw a boat gaining on them.

"Vander Norcross is onboard." Park smiled. "You aren't getting away this time."

There was a flash of fear on Olson's face before he hid it. "Norcross has gone soft." He rushed at Park.

Park blocked the kicks, but then Olson got a chop to his side.

His injured side.

Park stumbled, catching himself on the railing.

She scowled. Olson was fighting dirty.

She struggled with the ropes on her wrists. *Come on.* Finally, they loosened. *Yes.*

The ropes fell to the deck.

She ran and kicked Olson from behind. He spun and bared his teeth at her. He took a step toward her.

Park attacked him from behind.

Olson growled and spun. The men collided, straining against each other. She saw Olson reaching for his belt.

For the knife he had sheathed there.

No. Not happening.

Jenna leaped on Olson's back. She got her arm around his neck and started choking him.

The killer stepped back and rammed her against the pole she'd been tied to. Pain exploded along her shoulder blades, but she ignored it and held on.

He reached up and got a hand in her hair. He yanked her forward and over his shoulder.

Crap. She hit the deck flat on her back. The air rushed out of her and she groaned.

"You don't hurt her." Park charged, his face looking like death.

"I'll do whatever I want to her once you're dead."

A wave suddenly splashed over the side of the boat, and the men slipped on the wet deck. They fell to the ground, wrestling each other.

But she could see that they were evenly matched, and the water made the fight harder and slippery.

Jenna sat up and battled back a wave of dizziness.

She couldn't lose Park. She couldn't let him get hurt. He'd been through so much, and he deserved happiness.

He deserved to live.

Another wave crashed over the side, and she slid across the deck.

She reached out, trying to hold herself in place.

Her fingers closed over something.

The gun.

She whipped it up, and moved onto one knee. She aimed at the wet, wrestling men.

"Olson, let him go," she yelled.

"No!" the fugitive roared.

She didn't have a clear shot. With the boat rocking, she'd risk hitting Parker.

Park strained against Olson, then lifted his head and met her gaze.

"Do it," he said.

Her chest locked.

"I trust you, Jenna. Take the shot."

She pulled the trigger and fired.

CHAPTER EIGHTEEN

H e felt the heat of the bullet.

Park watched Olson slam back onto the deck. Jenna had shot him in the shoulder.

Olson snarled and shifted. She stepped forward and shot him in the other shoulder.

Park grinned at her. *God, she was something.* "I really like watching you work, Marshal Sheridan."

She smiled back at him. Her face was swollen, and it would bruise, but she'd never looked more beautiful to him.

He moved, ignoring the pain in his body. He then took great pleasure in tightening his fist and punching Olson in the face. The man flopped back on the deck with a low moan.

"That's for hitting her, asshole." Park punched him again. "That's because you deserve it."

Olson groaned.

"Park, as an officer of the law, I have to ask you to stop hitting the fugitive. Unfortunately."

He pulled some zip ties from his pocket. He roughly flipped Olson onto his stomach, and when the man made a pained sound, he didn't feel a lick of sympathy.

"Can't say I'm sorry, Olson." He fastened the man's ankles and wrists behind his back. He pulled the ties tight. He didn't give a fuck if he cut off Olson's circulation.

Jenna looked up at the helo and waved at Owen. The young marshal pumped his fist in the air.

There was a thud on the deck.

Shit, what now? Park crouched, ready for anything. He saw Jenna spin and lift her gun.

Two men in black wetsuits slid over the side of the boat.

Vander straightened, Ren beside him. Water sluiced off their bodies.

Vander eyed Olson, then looked up. "Looks like you didn't need our help."

Ren made a face. "You couldn't have saved anything for us?"

Park sat back against the railing, pain flaring inside him. He was pretty sure he had some broken ribs. "You guys were too slow. More than happy for you to take it from here, though."

Vander's lips quirked. "Congratulations, Jenna. You caught your fugitive."

She leaned against the boat controls. "Honestly, I'm just glad it's done."

Suddenly, Olson leaped up. He'd broken free of his ankle restraints. He sprinted for the side of the boat.

Ren cursed, and so did Park.

Vander moved faster than seemed possible. He gripped the back of Olson's neck, spun him, then slammed him face first into the railing of the boat. He yelped, blood pouring from his broken nose. Vander kicked the man's legs out from under him. He hit the deck hard.

"Ren, get a rope," Vander said calmly. "We'll hogtie him."

Jenna moved over to Park, weaving across the deck. She dropped down beside him. "You okay?"

"Yeah." He slid an arm around her. It hurt, but he wanted to hold her.

She leaned into him.

"You need ice on your face," he said.

"And you need ice on your ribs."

She hadn't missed that. He pressed a kiss to the top of her head.

Together, they watched Vander and Ren tie up Olson. This time, he wasn't getting loose.

It was done. It was over.

"You got your man," Park murmured.

She looked up. Her left eye was almost swollen shut. He gently touched her temple, and tucked her hair back behind her ear. How could she still smell so good after everything they'd been through today?

"I did. I found a hell of a man. Strong, tough, loyal. A good man, even though he doesn't think so."

Park's heart started pounding. "You aren't talking about Olson, right?"

"Very funny. I'd elbow you, but I know it would hurt." She shifted to look him directly in the eyes. "I know you don't want to hear this, Parker, but I'm falling in love with you."

He froze. He couldn't move, couldn't think. This gorgeous, smart woman loved him?

"I broke the rules. I promised you casual, but I'm not going to lie to you. I'm falling for you." Her nose wrinkled. "I'm really close to all the way in love."

"No."

Her eyebrow rose. "Yes."

Suddenly, the boat engine noise changed. He glanced over and saw Ren at the controls. The man worked on a research vessel and knew boats. He swung the boat around and pointed them back toward Valdez.

Park looked back at the woman staring at him. "You can't love me." Hell, his voice was shaky.

Her fingers curled on his forearm. "I do."

"You deserve better than me." She couldn't love him. She'd seen all his shadows, his scars, she'd seen all of him.

She made a sound. "Are you telling me I don't deserve a good man who respects me, likes my strength, has seen me cry, who has my back?"

Park swallowed.

"Who lights me up in bed."

He glanced up, and saw Ren and Vander watching them. Both the assholes were grinning.

Jenna touched his cheek and brought his gaze back to her.

"I'm falling crazily in love with you, Parker Conroy. So you're just going to have to deal with it."

His throat was too tight to talk. He pulled her against

his chest and held her tight. She rested her head on his shoulder.

"You deserve to be loved, Park. I'm going to prove that to you."

THE VALDEZ HARBOR WAS A ZOO. There were police and state troopers everywhere. An ambulance, plus the helicopter, sat on the street in front of the harbor. Curious onlookers stood on the sidewalk, pointing and speculating. Owen was directing things as best he could.

Jenna smiled as she scanned around her. Her partner was doing a hell of a job.

Olson was now shackled. There were four armed state troopers standing guard over him.

Vander and his guys had changed. They still looked badass. She'd never forget the moment when Vander and Ren had appeared on the boat.

She turned. Park was getting checked over by the paramedic. Though he was trying to push the guy away.

She stalked over. "Hey, I got checked over, and now it's your turn."

He glared at her. "Put that ice pack back on your face."

She held it up. "I will, if you let the nice paramedic check your ribs."

Park scowled, but unbuttoned his shirt. He winced, and it was obvious the stubborn man was in pain.

She pressed the ice pack back to her face. Nothing was broken, thankfully. She kept an eye on Park, on the man she loved, as the paramedic wrapped up his sore ribs.

Park kept glancing at her, like she might disappear.

Her scarred hero loved her. She knew it. He just didn't believe that he deserved to be loved back.

Well, she always got her man. She was going to make him realize that he deserved her and more.

Two black sedans sped down the street and screeched to a stop nearby. The doors opened, and when she saw the first man who stepped out, she stifled a groan.

Owen appeared beside her. "Incoming."

Typical Vic. Arriving when the hard work was all done, hoping to steal the glory.

Jenna didn't care. Olson was in custody, and she and Park were alive. That's all that mattered to her. That, and the fact that she'd finally discovered what true love felt like.

It wasn't all sweetness and warmth. It was intense, raw, and real.

"Thank you, everyone," Vic called out. "Your hard work in the apprehension of Kyle Olson has been invaluable."

Owen made a snorting sound.

The paramedic treating Park looked up. "Who's the blowhard?"

Now Jenna snorted. What had she ever seen in the man?

Vic spotted her and headed her way. He rested his hands on her shoulders. "Jenna, your face..."

She pulled back. "I'll live. You have good timing, Vic, as usual."

"You captured Olson. Well done, Jenna. I never doubted that you could take him down."

"I had help."

Vic took her hand and pulled her to the side. She really didn't want him touching her.

"I'm really impressed. You're a hell of a marshal."

"I know," she said dryly.

Vic's face suddenly changed. He touched her hair, a soft look in his eyes. "I miss you."

What? Her eyebrows winged up.

"I made a mistake with us, Jenna. With Mia. Things are not..." He shook his head. "I see now what a great team we were."

"A great team? Vic, you're married."

"I'm getting a divorce."

Jenna shook her head.

"Together, we could go places."

She made a sound. "So, I do all the dirty work, while you sit in your corner office, lapping up the credit?"

He frowned. "Jenna—"

"Look, Vic, I—"

She saw Vic look over her shoulder and his chest puffed up. She knew exactly who was behind her. She could sense Park blindfolded.

"Vic, this is Parker Conroy. He helped me catch Olson."

"The Army grunt." Vic crossed his arms. "Shame that you and your secret teams let someone like Olson loose."

Jenna made an annoyed sound. "Park doesn't run the entire military. He risked his life to help me bring Olson in. He hiked through the wilderness, he had my back, he protected and helped me. You know, did the dirty work."

Vic lifted his chin. "The US Marshals Service appreciates your help, Conroy. Now, we were having a private conversation—"

"No, we weren't," Jenna cut him off.

"Jenna, I messed up. I'm sorry."

"I doubt you are."

"That," Vic said. "I miss your toughness."

She crossed her arms. "I seem to recall you calling me a ballbuster."

Vic dragged in a breath. "I mean it, I miss you."

"Well, she doesn't miss you," Park said.

Vic's gaze narrowed. "What would you know?"

"Because she's been sleeping in my arms this week. She kisses me. She takes my cock. She loves me. She's *mine*."

Jenna's heart skipped a beat. She looked up at him, amused. "Is this some sort of alpha man claiming ritual?"

"No," Park said. "It's my claiming ritual."

She smiled at him.

"You're sleeping with...him," Vic spluttered. "I dated you for over a month and you wouldn't put out. But with *him*, it's only a few days."

"That's right, Vic."

"He's a killer." Vic stabbed a finger at Park. "He's just like Olson."

"He's nothing like Olson, and yes, I'm sleeping with him. I'm in love with him."

Park cupped her cheeks. "Go away, Vic."

Vic grumbled. "You're making a mistake, Jenna."

"No, you were a mistake." She didn't even look at him. All she could see was Park. "Thankfully, you were a short-lived, easily forgotten one."

Her ex huffed. "You'll regret this." He stalked off.

"No, I won't." She gripped Park's wrists. "Yours, huh?"

"Yes. I'm not really good with words, so let me show you how I feel." He lowered his head and claimed her mouth with his.

JENNA CLUNG to Park as he kissed her.

He hauled her closer and kissed her like he never wanted to stop.

He still couldn't believe she loved him. Couldn't find the right words to share how he felt.

A clearing throat made him lift his head. He looked over and saw Vander and the others standing there, smiling at them.

"Olson's gone," Vander said.

Park tucked Jenna against him, and they both looked at the street. The car the marshals had loaded Olson into was driving away, red taillights glowing. It was escorted by both marshals and state troopers.

Olson wouldn't be escaping this time.

"Good riddance," Jenna murmured.

Vander gripped Park's shoulder. "Well done. Both of you."

"He didn't make it easy," Park said. "He hurt a lot of people."

"But he can't hurt anyone ever again," Jenna said.

Park knew she was thinking of her father.

"Jenna," a voice called out.

Owen stood nearby with some state troopers, waving at her.

She squeezed Park's arm. "I need to deal with this."

He watched her walk over to the group. Then he watched the way they listened to her, and he felt proud as hell.

"You helped Jenna stop Olson," Vander said. "You saved lives, Park."

"Thanks for coming." Vander was one of the people Park trusted most. He knew the man would always have his back.

Park realized that he wasn't as isolated as he'd thought. He saw Boone, Shep, and Ren nearby. His friends, his brothers. Loyalty was in their marrow.

And Park would return the favor if they ever needed him.

"You didn't really need us," Vander said. "You and Jenna make a hell of a team."

"She's in love with me."

"Then that makes you a lucky man."

"I know."

Park knew he could go back to his cabin. He could avoid people, avoid life...

But she'd changed him. No, maybe she'd just pulled the blinders off so he could see more clearly.

"I don't deserve her. I'm not good enough for her."

Vander smiled. "You're not, but she chose you. She loves you. You think you can walk away and let her go?"

Park looked over at her. She was waving a hand as she talked. "Fuck, no."

"Good. I was worried I was going to have to knock some sense into you. You have a lifetime to do everything you can to make her happy. All you have to do is love her."

Vander sounded like he was speaking from experience.

Park dragged in a deep breath. "Shit." A shot of fear hit him. A part of him would prefer to take on a pack of Olsons.

Vander's smile widened. "I know the feeling. We've all been there." He nodded at the others. "I get how it feels to think you're not good enough for your woman, to feel that you don't know how to love her. She'll help you. She'll show you." An amused look across Vander's face. "And she'll let you know when you get it wrong."

Park let out a low laugh.

"It's good to hear that. You deserve the happiness, Park."

"Thanks, Vander. For everything."

He slapped Park on the back. "Always. We're Ghost Ops. We've been to hell together, and no matter when or where, we're always there for each other."

Park looked over at his friends. Boone nodded, Shep shot him a salute, and Ren grinned.

"And if you ever want a job, you've always got one with Norcross Security," Vander added.

"Thanks."

"Now, go and get your woman."

Park walked over to Jenna. She looked up, and he

hated seeing the swelling and developing bruises on her face. She looked tired.

Most of all, she couldn't hide the uncertainty in her eyes.

"Hey," she said.

"Hey." He stopped, with only inches between them.

"Olson's gone," she said. "He'll die in prison."

"He will." He touched her face. "I could've killed him for this."

"No killing. I don't want to have to arrest you." She swallowed. "Are you leaving with Vander and the others?"

"No. Are you leaving? Going back to Virginia?"

"No."

He cocked his head. "No?"

"I asked for some time off. To recover."

His heart kicked in his chest. "What are your plans for your time off?"

"Well, I was hoping there might be a nice cabin somewhere, with some peace and quiet where I can relax and recuperate."

He wrapped his arms around her. "I might know a place."

"Really?"

"It includes decent food and amazing sex."

"Amazing, huh?" She smiled.

He pulled in a breath. "It also includes a man who loves you."

She stilled.

"A man who doesn't deserve a woman like you—"

She pressed a finger to his lips. "Quiet. This woman

disagrees. She sees a hero. One she can trust in every way. One who'll never lie or betray her." She paused. "You didn't want to fall in love."

"I know. But you changed everything. I love you, Jenna."

Warmth filled her face. "I love you too, Park." She went up on her toes and kissed him. "Now take me home."

CHAPTER NINETEEN

Jenna spun on the couch, laughing. "*No*."

Behind her, Park sank his teeth into her bare buttock. Her laughter increased, as did the electric sensations skating through her body.

He just finished fucking her brains out on the couch, so she shouldn't feel desire like this again so soon.

They'd been watching a movie, but things had escalated.

He reached down and tickled behind her knee. Her secret ticklish spot that he'd recently discovered. He'd spent the last week learning and memorizing every part of her body.

"No," she cried again. She rolled, and they overbalanced. They both tipped off the couch and landed on the floor. Of course, Park being Park, moved fast and landed first, breaking her fall.

"Your ribs—"

"Are fine," he assured her.

They'd been at his cabin for a week. He'd healed fast

and was moving better. He'd proven that by fucking her in every room of the cabin, on just about every surface. Meanwhile, her bruises were a lovely puce color.

One day, they'd driven to Drifter Lake Lodge. They'd collected the rest of their things, and explained to Velma and Ross who they really were. When they'd talked about the Hoskins, Velma had cried on Jenna's shoulder, and thanked her for getting justice for their friends. The couple had invited them back anytime.

Park kissed her, cupping the back of her head. The kiss was fierce, possessive, and filled with love.

Saying the words was hard for him, but he'd showed her every day what he felt for her. He worshiped her, took care of her. This man held her heart.

But worry niggled at her. He'd come to Alaska for peace and solitude...but her life was back in Virginia. She loved her job and her work was important to her.

She couldn't stay in this cabin, isolated from the world, no matter how much she loved him.

"Hungry?" He rose, so at ease with his nakedness.

"I could eat."

Park helped her to her feet, then pressed a quick kiss to the healing graze on her head. He pulled on his jeans, and she nabbed his T-shirt and slipped it over her head. She watched him putter around the kitchen, shirtless.

Mmm. She could watch him all day.

When he put some food on a small plate, she hid her smile. She followed him onto the deck and watched as he set the plate down by the steps. A ritual she'd seen him do every day.

Turned out that her man was a softy underneath the intense, grouchy badass.

He saw her face and she couldn't hide her smile anymore.

"He might get hungry if I don't feed him," Park said defensively.

The squirrel appeared, skittering along the railing, then attacking the plate of food.

"He's a squirrel, Park."

"Yeah, but you never know." He glanced down. "Red, have some manners."

The animal had scattered food everywhere.

She walked over and leaned against Park's back, enjoying his warm skin.

He reached back and touched her. "Something's bothering you." He turned to face her.

"No. I love it here. You picked a great spot."

He cupped the uninjured side of her face. "I've become an expert in all your facial expressions. When you're happy, aroused, calm, stressed... And worried."

She blew out a breath. Damn him for reading her so easily. "I love being with you. This week... It's been perfect."

She felt the tension fill his body. "But?"

"There is no but."

"There is. Jenna—"

She met his gold-brown gaze head on. "I love you, Parker."

A muscle in his jaw ticked. "I love you too. More than I ever thought possible."

"I also love my job."

"And you're damn good at it. You put people like Olson away. The world needs you."

"I can't do it here," she whispered, her fingers digging into his skin.

His lips quirked. "I know."

"I want to be with you. And not just sometimes, or on the odd vacation. I want to be with you every day. I want to know I'm coming home to you."

"I want that as well." He pulled her closer. "That's why I'm coming with you."

She blinked. "What?"

"I want you to come home to me every day. I want you to sleep in my arms every night. I...came here to hide. I thought this place would give me peace. The only real peace I've found is when I'm with you."

Warmth wrapped around her heart. "Park—"

"I'm coming with you. We'll make a life together, our way. I don't need to hide in the dark anymore."

She grinned, unable to hold her happiness in. "We're doing this?"

"Yes."

She squealed, then jumped up and wrapped her legs around his waist. His hand slid under her ass.

"Have I mentioned how much I love you?" She attacked his neck with her mouth. She barely registered his scars under her lips. They were a part of him. A part of the man she loved.

He arched his head. "I'm not going to stop from you telling me over and over again." He carried her toward the door. Then he stumbled and cursed.

She tightened her hold on him. "Park?"

"Damn you, Red." Park lifted his foot. "He moved the plate right where I would step on it. I swear that squirrel is trying to kill me."

"We'll keep the cabin," she said. "We'll come here for our vacations and visit Red."

Park smiled. "Yeah. And so I have a place where I can keep my beautiful marshal naked all the time." His mouth devoured hers.

She nipped his bottom lip. "I like the sound of that."

"Good." He headed for the bedroom. "Because I plan to get you naked now."

A few months later

"RESERVATION FOR CONROY."

The hostess at the Waterbar Restaurant in San Franciso smiled and nodded. "This way, sir."

She led Park to a table by the windows and he ordered a bourbon. Then he looked out the glass at the stellar view of the Bay Bridge. The lights on it sparkled in the night sky.

He and Jenna lived in San Francisco now. Jenna had gotten a transfer with the Marshal Service to the San Francisco office. And Parker had taken a job at Norcross Security.

He loved it. The job had variety and was generally safe. He got to help people without the work stealing his soul.

He got to see Vander every day and he'd made friends with the other Norcross employees.

And he was close to his woman if she needed him.

He and Jenna had pooled their resources and bought a house that backed onto the Presidio. She'd told him that she didn't want him to feel hemmed in by the city. At their home, he could look out the window and see trees. When he needed space, he could run in the park.

He loved their life here. The life they were making together.

Tonight, he had something else for her. He touched the small box resting in his pocket.

Shit, he felt exactly how he did before a dangerous mission.

Then he saw her.

She'd changed. When she'd left for work this morning, she'd been wearing dark jeans and a suede jacket. She was now wearing a killer little black dress that ended at her knees and had a neckline that plunged in a deep V. Her blonde hair was loose, and she looked gorgeous.

A man at a nearby table turned to watch her walk past, smiling with appreciation.

Park glared at the man, and sensing something, the man looked over. When he met Park's gaze, the man quickly turned back to his food.

"Are you intimidating people?" Jenna stopped beside him. "You've got your badass face on."

He rose and pulled her close. "I'm only intimidating men who are looking at what's mine."

His lips touched hers and she opened for him. He kissed her deeply, loving the husky sound she made.

"I only have eyes for you, Park," she murmured, a little breathless.

"Good." He held out a chair for her.

She sat. "I love the view."

He kept his gaze on her. "Me too."

Her lips twitched. "Look at you with the charm."

"How was work?"

"Good. I caught some bad guys. You?"

"Same. Caught some bad guys." He couldn't wait any longer. He reached across the table and took her hand. "Jenna?"

Her brow creased, her fingers twining with his. "What's wrong?"

"Nothing." He swallowed. "Nothing at all. Everything's right whenever I'm with you." He slipped his hand into his pocket, then set the box in the middle of the table between them.

Her chest hitched and she stared at the box. "I know you're a man of action, Park, but I need some words right now."

There was a flush in her cheeks and her eyes were alight with love.

She loved him. It still amazed him.

He flicked the box open. "Jenna, I love you. You're it for me, and every day, you make my world a better place. Will you marry me? Will you be mine? Always."

She pressed her other hand over his. "Yes, because I'm already yours." She wiggled her fingers. "Put it on."

"I wanted to get you a ring that wouldn't get in your way. That you can wear to work." The ring was two bands of glittering diamonds twisted together. There was no large stone to snag on anything. He slid it onto her finger.

Shit, his hands were shaking.

"I love it. I love you." She rose and Park pushed his chair back. He pulled her onto his lap. He didn't care that they were in the middle of a restaurant.

"Mine," he murmured.

"Yours."

He was still kissing her when screams broke out, and glass shattered on the floor.

Jenna jerked.

Park looked up and saw two men wearing balaclavas storm into the restaurant. One was holding a shotgun and the other a handgun.

"We want everyone's phones, wallets, and jewelry," one man yelled, opening a black sack. "Put everything in here, and no one gets hurt."

Jenna's gaze narrowed. "These two picked the wrong place."

Park hid a smile. "They sure did. I love watching my kickass marshal in action."

She patted his jaw. "I love having my badass man as my backup."

They waited until the men closed in on their table. Jenna morphed into a terrified woman. "Oh my God, please don't hurt us!"

"Just hand over your stuff." The man shook the sack. "Now!"

Jenna squeezed Park's leg, indicating which guy she was going for. The one with the sack.

That left shotgun guy for him. *Good.*

Jenna rose. "Oh, God. Oh, God."

Jeez, she was good. If he didn't know her, he'd believe she was terrified.

"Put it all in the bag." The man held the sack out.

Jenna stood. "I don't think so." She took a step, grabbed the bag, and twisted it, tangling it around the man's arm.

His brows snapped together. "Hey—"

She rammed her leg up, kneeing him between the legs. He let out a sound that made Park wince.

The other man started to move. Park attacked. He shot out of his chair and yanked the shotgun out of the man's hands. He whirled it around and rammed the butt of the shotgun into the man's gut. He doubled over with a loud *oof*, and Park gripped the back of his neck and slammed his face into the table. The plates and cutlery rattled.

The man let out a gurgle and dropped to the floor.

Jenna drove her guy to his knees.

"US Marshal, asshole. You're under arrest." She raised her head. "Someone call 911, please."

"On it," a man said, fumbling for his cellphone.

The restaurant broke out in cheers and applause.

A man in a suit, the restaurant manager, hurried over. "Thank you. Thank you so much!"

"I'm US Marshal Jenna Sheridan. And this is... my fiancé, Parker. We just got engaged, and I wasn't planning to hand over my new engagement ring to these guys." She held out her hand to show the man.

The manager smiled. "It's a lovely ring. After the

police have dealt with these men, your dinner and drinks are on the house."

She smiled. "Thanks."

"Oh, and congratulations, to both of you," the manager added.

Jenna stepped over one of the whimpering bad guys and kissed Park. He pulled her close.

"We'll have to make dinner quick," she said, "because I have the urge to get home and fuck my fiancé."

A shot of heat punched into his gut. He couldn't love her more. She was his perfect match. She was the perfect blend of beauty, smart, toughness, and sexiness.

"And I can't wait to fuck my fiancée," he replied.

She smiled at him with love on her face, and Park thanked whatever gods had sent her his way. A part of him was damn glad Olson had run off to Alaska and brought Jenna Sheridan knocking on Park's door.

She'd pulled him out of the shadows, she'd given him peace, and now he'd spend every day of his life loving her.

I hope you enjoyed Parker and Jenna's story! Thank you so much for loving these Unbroken Heroes as much as I have.

Look out for my brand-new series, **Langston Hotels,** coming in May 2025.

If you'd like to know more about **Vander Norcross**

and his team, then check out the first Norcross Security book, *The Investigator,* starring Rhys Norcross. **Read on for a preview of the first chapter.**

Don't miss out! For updates about new releases, free books, and other fun stuff, sign up for my VIP mailing list and get your *free box set* containing three action-packed romances.

Visit here to get started: www.annahackett.com

Would you like
a FREE BOX SET
of my books?

There was a glass of chardonnay with her name on it waiting for her at home.

Haven McKinney smiled. The museum was closed, and she was *done* for the day.

As she walked across the East gallery of the Hutton Museum, her heels clicked on the marble floor.

God, she loved the place. The creamy marble that made up the flooring and wrapped around the grand pillars was gorgeous. It had that hushed air of grandeur that made her heart squeeze a little every time she stepped inside. But more than that, the amazing art the Hutton housed sang to the art lover in her blood.

Snagging a job here as the curator six months ago had been a dream come true. She'd been at a low point in her life. Very low. Haven swallowed a snort and circled a stunning white-marble sculpture of a naked, reclining woman with the most perfect resting bitch face. She'd never guessed that her life would come crashing down at age twenty-nine.

She lifted her chin. Miami was her past. The Hutton and San Francisco were her future. No more throwing caution to the wind. She had a plan, and she was sticking to it.

She paused in front of a stunning exhibit of traditional Chinese painting and calligraphy. It was one of their newer exhibits, and had been Haven's brainchild. Nearby, an interactive display was partially assembled. Over the next few days, her staff would finish the installation. Excitement zipped through Haven. She couldn't wait to have the touchscreens operational. It was her passion to make art more accessible, especially to children. To help them be a part of it, not just look at it. To learn, to feel, to enjoy.

Art had helped her through some of the toughest times in her life, and she wanted to share that with others.

She looked at the gorgeous old paintings again. One portrayed a mountainous landscape with beautiful maple trees. It soothed her nerves.

Wine would soothe her nerves, as well. *Right*. She

needed to get upstairs to her office and grab her handbag, then get an Uber home.

Her cell phone rang and she unclipped it from the lanyard she wore at the museum. "Hello?"

"Change of plans, girlfriend," a smoky female voice said. "Let's go out and celebrate being gorgeous, successful, and single. I'm done at the office, and believe me, it has been a *grueling* day."

Haven smiled at her new best friend. She'd met Gia Norcross when she joined the Hutton. Gia's wealthy brother, Easton Norcross, owned the museum, and was Haven's boss. The museum was just a small asset in the businessman's empire. Haven suspected Easton owned at least a third of San Francisco. Maybe half.

She liked and respected her boss. Easton could be tough, but he valued her opinions. And she loved his bossy, take-charge, energetic sister. Gia ran a highly successful PR firm in the city, and did all the PR and advertising for the Hutton. They'd met not long after Haven had started work at the museum.

After their first meeting, Gia had dragged Haven out to her favorite restaurant and bar, and the rest was history.

"I guess making people's Instagram look pretty and not staged is hard work," Haven said with a grin.

"Bitch." Gia laughed. "God, I had a meeting with a businessman caught in...well, let's just say he and his assistant were *not* taking notes on the boardroom table."

Haven felt an old, unwelcome memory rise up. She mentally stomped it down. "I don't feel sorry for the cheating asshole, I feel sorry for whatever poor shmuck got more than they were paid for when they walked into the boardroom."

"Actually, it was the cheating businessman's wife."

"Uh-oh."

"And the assistant was male," Gia added.

"Double uh-oh."

"Then said cheater comes to my PR firm, telling me to clean up his mess, because he's thinking he might run for governor one day. I mean, I'm good, but I can't wrangle miracles."

Haven suspected that Gia had verbally eviscerated the man and sent him on his way. Gia Norcross had a sharp tongue, and wasn't afraid to use it.

"So, grueling day and I need alcohol. I'll meet you at ONE65, and the first drink is on me."

"I'm pretty wiped, Gia—"

"Uh-uh, no excuses. I'll see you in an hour." And with that, Gia was gone.

Haven clipped her phone to her lanyard. Well, it looked like she was having that chardonnay at ONE65, the six-story, French dining experience Gia loved. Each level offered something different, from patisserie, to bistro and grill, to bar and lounge.

Haven walked into the museum's main gallery, and her blood pressure dropped to a more normal level. It was her favorite space in the museum. The smell of wood, the gorgeous lights gleaming overhead, and the amazing paintings combined to create a soothing room. She smoothed her hands down her fitted, black skirt. Haven was tall, at five foot eight, and curvy, just like her mom had been. Her boobs, currently covered by a cute, white blouse with a tie around her neck, weren't much to write home about, but she had to buy her skirts one size bigger. She sighed. No matter how much she walked or jogged —*blergh*, okay, she didn't jog much—she still had an ass.

Even in her last couple of months in Miami, when stress had caused her to lose a bunch of weight due to everything going on, her ass hadn't budged.

Memories of Miami—and her douchebag-of-epic-proportions-ex—threatened, churning like storm clouds on the horizon.

Nope. She locked those thoughts down. She was *not* going there.

She had a plan, and the number one thing for taking back and rebuilding her life was *no* men. She'd sworn off anyone with a Y chromosome.

She didn't need one, didn't want one, she was D-O-N-E, done.

She stopped in front of the museum's star attraction. Claude Monet's *Water Lilies*.

Haven loved the impressionist's work. She loved the colors, the delicate strokes. This one depicted water lilies and lily pads floating on a gentle pond. His paintings always made an impact, and had a haunting, yet soothing feel to them.

It was also worth just over a hundred million dollars.

The price tag still made her heart flutter. She'd put a business case to Easton, and they'd purchased the painting three weeks ago at auction. Haven had planned out the display down to the rivets used on the wood. She'd thrown herself into the project.

Gia had put together a killer marketing campaign,

and Haven had reluctantly been interviewed by the local paper. But it had paid off. Ticket sales to the museum were up, and everyone wanted to see *Water Lilies*.

Footsteps echoed through the empty museum, and she turned to see a uniformed security guard appear in the doorway.

"Ms. McKinney?"

"Yes, David? I was just getting ready to leave."

"Sorry to delay you. There's a delivery truck at the back entrance. They say they have a delivery of a Zadkine bronze."

Haven frowned, running through the next day's schedule in her head. "That's due tomorrow."

"It sounds like they had some other deliveries nearby and thought they'd squeeze it in."

She glanced at her slim, silver wristwatch, fighting back annoyance. She'd had a long day, and now she'd be late to meet Gia. "Fine. Have them bring it in."

With a nod, David disappeared. Haven pulled out her phone and quickly fired off a text to warn Gia that she'd be late. Then Haven headed up to her office, and checked her notes for tomorrow. She had several calls to make to chase down some pieces for a new exhibit she wanted to launch in the winter. There were some restoration quotes to go over, and a charity gala for her art charity to plan. She needed to get down into the storage rooms and see if there was anything they could cycle out and put on display.

God, she loved her job. Not many people would get excited about digging around in dusty storage rooms, but Haven couldn't wait.

She made sure her laptop was off and grabbed her handbag. She slipped her lanyard off and stuffed her phone in her bag.

When she reached the bottom of the stairs, she heard a strange noise from the gallery. A muffled pop, then a thump.

Frowning, she took one step toward the gallery.

Suddenly, David staggered through the doorway, a splotch of red on his shirt.

Haven's pulse spiked. *Oh God, was that blood?* "David—"

"Run." He collapsed to the floor.

Fear choking her, she kicked off her heels and spun. She had to get help.

But she'd only taken two steps when a hand sank into her hair, pulling her neat twist loose, and sending her brown hair cascading over her shoulders.

"Let me go!"

She was dragged into the main gallery, and when she lifted her head, her gut churned.

Five men dressed in black, all wearing balaclavas, stood in a small group.

No...oh, no.

Their other guard, Gus, stood with his hands in the air. He was older, former military. She was shoved closer toward him.

"Ms. McKinney, you okay?" Gus asked.

She managed a nod. "They shot David."

"I kn—"

"No talking," one man growled.

Haven lifted her chin. "What do you want?" There was a slight quaver in her voice.

The man who'd grabbed her glared. His cold, blue eyes glittered through the slits in his balaclava. Then he ignored her, and with the others, they turned to face the *Water Lilies*.

Haven's stomach dropped. *No.* This couldn't be happening.

A thin man moved forward, studying the painting's gilt frame with gloved hands. "It's wired to an alarm."

Blue Eyes, clearly the group's leader, turned and aimed the gun at Gus' barrel chest. "Disconnect it."

"No," the guard said belligerently.

"I'm not asking."

Haven held up her hands. "Please—"

The gun fired. Gus dropped to one knee, pressing a hand to his shoulder.

"No!" she cried.

The leader stepped forward and pressed the gun to the older man's head.

"No." Haven fought back her fear and panic. "Don't hurt him. I'll disconnect it."

Slowly, she inched toward the painting, carefully avoiding the thin man still standing close to it. She touched the security panel built in beside the frame, pressing her palm to the small pad.

A second later, there was a discreet beep.

Two other men came forward and grabbed the frame.

She glanced around at them. "You're making a mistake. If you know who owns this museum, then you know you won't get away with this." Who would go up against the Norcross family? Easton, rich as sin, had a lot of connections, but his brother, Vander... Haven suppressed a shiver. Gia's middle brother might be hot, but he scared the bejesus out of Haven.

Vander Norcross, former military badass, owned Norcross Security and Investigations. His team had put in the high-tech security for the museum.

No one in their right mind wanted to go up against Vander, or the third Norcross brother who also worked with Vander, or the rest of Vander's team of badasses.

"Look, if you just—"

The blow to her head made her stagger. She blinked, pain radiating through her face. Blue Eyes had back-handed her.

He moved in and hit her again, and Haven cried out, clutching her face. It wasn't the first time she'd been hit. Her douchebag ex had hit her once. That was the day she'd left him for good.

But this was worse. Way worse.

"Shut up, you stupid bitch."

The next blow sent her to the floor. She thought she heard someone chuckle. He followed with a kick to her ribs, and Haven curled into a ball, a sob in her throat.

Her vision wavered and she blinked. Blue Eyes crouched down, putting his hand to the tiles right in front of her. Dizziness hit her, and she vaguely took in the freckles on the man's hand. They formed a spiral pattern.

"No one talks back to me," the man growled. "Especially a woman." He moved away.

She saw the men were busy maneuvering the painting off the wall. It was easy for two people to move.

She knew its exact dimensions—eighty by one hundred centimeters.

No one was paying any attention to her. Fighting through the nausea and dizziness, she dragged herself a few inches across the floor, closer to the nearby pillar. A pillar that had one of several hidden, high-tech panic buttons built into it.

When the men were turned away, she reached up and pressed the button.

Then blackness sucked her under.

HAVEN SAT on one of the lovely wooden benches she'd had installed around the museum. She'd wanted somewhere for guests to sit and take in the art.

She'd never expected to be sitting on one, holding a melting ice pack to her throbbing face, and staring at the empty wall where a multi-million-dollar masterpiece should be hanging. And she definitely didn't expect to be doing it with police dusting black powder all over the museum's walls.

Tears pricked her eyes. She was alive, her guards were hurt but alive, and that was what mattered. The police had questioned her and she'd told them everything she could remember. The paramedics had checked her over and given her the ice pack. Nothing was broken, but she'd been told to expect swelling and bruising.

David and Gus had been taken to the hospital. She'd been assured the men would be okay. Last she'd heard, David was in surgery. Her throat tightened. *Oh, God.*

What was she going to tell Easton?

Haven bit her lip and a tear fell down her cheek. She hadn't cried in months. She'd shed more than enough tears over Leo after he'd gone crazy and hit her. She'd left Miami the next day. She'd needed to get away from her ex and, unfortunately, despite loving her job at a classy Miami art gallery, Leo's cousin had owned it. Alyssa had been the one who had introduced them.

Haven had learned a painful lesson to not mix business and pleasure.

She'd been done with Leo's growing moodiness, outbursts, and cheating on her and hitting her had been the last straw. *Asshole.*

She wiped the tear away. San Francisco was as far from Miami as she could get and still be in the continental US. This was supposed to be her fresh new start.

She heard footsteps—solid, quick, and purposeful. Easton strode in.

He was a tall man, with dark hair that curled at the collar of his perfectly fitted suit. Haven had sworn off men, but she was still woman enough to appreciate her boss' good looks. His mother was Italian-American, and she'd passed down her very good genes to her children.

Like his brothers, Easton had been in the military, too, although he'd joined the Army Rangers. It showed in his muscled body. Once, she'd seen his shirt sleeves rolled up when they'd had a late meeting. He had some interesting ink that was totally at odds with his sophisticated-businessman persona.

His gaze swept the room, his jaw tight. It settled on her and he strode over.

"Haven—"

"Oh God, Easton. I'm so sorry."

He sat beside her and took her free hand. He squeezed her cold fingers, then he looked at her face and cursed.

She hadn't been brave enough to look in the mirror, but she guessed it was bad.

"They took the *Water Lilies*," she said.

"Okay, don't worry about it just now."

She gave a hiccupping laugh. "Don't worry? It's worth a hundred and ten *million* dollars."

A muscle ticked in his jaw. "You're okay, and that's the main thing. And the guards are in serious but stable condition at the hospital."

She nodded numbly. "It's all my fault."

Easton's gaze went to the police, and then moved back to her. "That's not true."

"I let them in." Her voice broke. God, she wanted the marble floor to crack and swallow her.

"Don't worry." Easton's face turned very serious. "Vander and Rhys will find the painting."

Her boss' tone made her shiver. Something made her suspect that Easton wanted his brothers to find the men who'd stolen the painting more than recovering the price-less piece of art.

She licked her lips, and felt the skin on her cheek tug. She'd have some spectacular bruises later. *Great. Thanks, universe.*

Then Easton's head jerked up, and Haven followed his gaze.

A man stood in the doorway. She hadn't heard him

coming. Nope, Vander Norcross moved silently, like a ghost.

He was a few inches over six feet, had a powerful body, and radiated authority. His suit didn't do much to tone down the sense that a predator had stalked into the room. While Easton was handsome, Vander wasn't. His face was too rugged, and while both he and Easton had blue eyes, Vander's were dark indigo, and as cold as the deepest ocean depths.

He didn't look happy. She fought back a shiver.

Then another man stepped up beside Vander.

Haven's chest locked. *Oh, no. No, no, no.*

She should have known. He was Vander's top investigator. Rhys Matteo Norcross, the youngest of the Norcross brothers.

At first glance, he looked like his brothers—similar build, muscular body, dark hair and bronze skin. But Rhys was the youngest, and he had a charming edge his brothers didn't share. He smiled more frequently, and his shaggy, thick hair always made her imagine him as a rock star, holding a guitar and making girls scream.

Haven was also totally, one hundred percent in lust with him. Any time he got near, he made her body flare to life, her heart beat faster, and made her brain freeze up. She could barely talk around the man.

She did *not* want Rhys Norcross to notice her. Or talk to her. Or turn his soulful, brown eyes her way.

Nuh-uh. No way. She'd sworn off men. This one should have a giant warning sign hanging on him. *Watch out, heartbreak waiting to happen.*

Rhys had been in the military with Vander. Some

hush-hush special unit that no one talked about. Now he worked at Norcross Security—apparently finding anything and anyone.

He also raced cars and boats in his free time. The man liked to go fast. Oh, and he bedded women. His reputation was legendary. Rhys liked a variety of adventures and experiences.

It was lucky Haven had sworn off men.

Especially when they happened to be her boss' brother.

And especially, especially when they were also her best friend's brother.

Off limits.

She saw the pair turn to look her and Easton's way.

Crap. Pulse racing, she looked at her bare feet and red toenails, which made her realize she hadn't recovered her shoes yet. They were her favorites.

She felt the men looking at her, and like she was drawn by a magnet, she looked up. Vander was scowling. Rhys' dark gaze was locked on her.

Haven's traitorous heart did a little tango in her chest.

Before she knew what was happening, Rhys went down on one knee in front of her.

She saw rage twist his handsome features. Then he shocked her by cupping her jaw, and pushing the ice pack away.

They'd never talked much. At Gia's parties, Haven purposely avoided him. He'd never touched her before, and she felt the warmth of him singe through her.

His eyes flashed. "It's going to be okay, baby."

Baby?

He stroked her cheekbone, those long fingers gentle.

Fighting for some control, Haven closed her hand over his wrist. She swallowed. "I—"

"Don't worry, Haven. I'm going to find the man who did this to you and make him regret it."

Her belly tightened. *Oh, God.* When was the last time anyone had looked out for her like this? She was certain no one had ever promised to hunt anyone down for her. Her gaze dropped to his lips.

He had amazingly shaped lips, a little fuller than such a tough man should have, framed by dark stubble.

There was a shift in his eyes and his face warmed. His fingers kept stroking her skin and she felt that caress all over.

Then she heard the click of heels moving at speed. Gia burst into the room.

"What the hell is going on?"

Haven jerked back from Rhys and his hypnotic touch. Damn, she'd been proven right—she was so weak where this man was concerned.

Gia hurried toward them. She was five-foot-four, with a curvy, little body, and a mass of dark, curly hair. As usual, she wore one of her power suits—short skirt, fitted jacket, and sky-high heels.

"Out of my way." Gia shouldered Rhys aside. When her friend got a look at Haven, her mouth twisted. "I'm going to *kill* them."

"Gia," Vander said. "The place is filled with cops. Maybe keep your plans for murder and vengeance quiet."

"Fix this." She pointed at Vander's chest, then at

Rhys. Then she turned and hugged Haven. "You're coming home with me."

"Gia—"

"No. No arguments." Gia held up her palm like a traffic cop. Haven had seen "the hand" before. It was pointless arguing.

Besides, she realized she didn't want to be alone. And the quicker she got away from Rhys' dark, far-too-perceptive gaze, the better.

Norcross Security
The Investigator
The Troubleshooter
The Specialist
The Bodyguard
The Hacker
The Powerbroker
The Detective
The Medic
The Protector
Also Available as Audiobooks!

PREVIEW: TREASURE HUNTER SECURITY

Want to learn more about *Treasure Hunter Security*? Check out the first book in the series, *Undiscovered*, Declan Ward's action-packed story.

One former Navy SEAL. One dedicated archeologist. One secret map to a fabulous lost oasis.

Finding undiscovered treasures is always daring,

dangerous, and deadly. Perfect for the men of Treasure Hunter Security. Former Navy SEAL Declan Ward is haunted by the demons of his past and throws everything he has into his security business—Treasure Hunter Security. Dangerous archeological digs – no problem. Daring expeditions – sure thing. Museum security for invaluable exhibits – easy. But on a simple dig in the Egyptian desert, he collides with a stubborn, smart archeologist, Dr. Layne Rush, and together they get swept into a deadly treasure hunt for a mythical lost oasis. When an evil from his past reappears, Declan vows to do anything to protect Layne.

Dr. Layne Rush is dedicated to building a successful career—a promise to the parents she lost far too young. But when her dig is plagued by strange accidents, targeted by a lethal black market antiquities ring, and artifacts are stolen, she is forced to turn to Treasure Hunter Security, and to the tough, sexy, and too-used-to-giving-orders Declan. Soon her organized dig morphs into a wild treasure hunt across the desert dunes.

Danger is hunting them every step of the way, and Layne and Declan must find a way to work together...to not only find the treasure but to survive.

Treasure Hunter Security
Undiscovered
Uncharted
Unexplored
Unfathomed
Untraveled

Unmapped
Unidentified
Undetected
Also Available as Audiobooks!

Stone

Also Available as Audiobooks!

Norcross Security

The Investigator

The Troubleshooter

The Specialist

The Bodyguard

The Hacker

The Powerbroker

The Detective

The Medic

The Protector

Mr. & Mrs. Norcross

Also Available as Audiobooks!

Billionaire Heists

Stealing from Mr. Rich

Blackmailing Mr. Bossman

Hacking Mr. CEO

Also Available as Audiobooks!

Team 52

Mission: Her Protection

Mission: Her Rescue

Mission: Her Security

Mission: Her Defense

Mission: Her Safety

Mission: Her Freedom

Mission: Her Shield

Mission: Her Justice

Also Available as Audiobooks!

Treasure Hunter Security

Undiscovered

Uncharted

Unexplored

Unfathomed

Untraveled

Unmapped

Unidentified

Undetected

Also Available as Audiobooks!

Oronis Knights

Knightmaster

Knighthunter

Galactic Kings

Overlord

Emperor

Captain of the Guard

Conqueror

Also Available as Audiobooks!

Eon Warriors

Edge of Eon

Touch of Eon

Heart of Eon

Kiss of Eon

Mark of Eon

Claim of Eon

Storm of Eon

Soul of Eon

King of Eon

Also Available as Audiobooks!

Galactic Gladiators: House of Rone

Sentinel

Defender

Centurion

Paladin

Guard

Weapons Master

Also Available as Audiobooks!

Galactic Gladiators

Gladiator

Warrior

Hero

Protector

Champion

Barbarian

Beast

Rogue

Guardian

Cyborg

Imperator

Hunter

Also Available as Audiobooks!

Hell Squad

Marcus

Cruz

Gabe

Reed

Roth

Noah

Shaw

Holmes

Niko

Finn

Devlin

Theron

Hemi

Ash

Levi

Manu

Griff

Dom

Survivors

Tane

Also Available as Audiobooks!

The Anomaly Series

Time Thief

Mind Raider

Soul Stealer

Salvation

Anomaly Series Box Set

The Phoenix Adventures

Among Galactic Ruins

At Star's End

In the Devil's Nebula

On a Rogue Planet

Beneath a Trojan Moon

Beyond Galaxy's Edge

On a Cyborg Planet

Return to Dark Earth

On a Barbarian World

Lost in Barbarian Space

Through Uncharted Space

Crashed on an Ice World

Perma Series

Winter Fusion

A Galactic Holiday

Warriors of the Wind

Tempest

Storm & Seduction

Fury & Darkness

Standalone Titles

Savage Dragon

Hunter's Surrender

One Night with the Wolf

For more information visit www.annahackett.com

ABOUT THE AUTHOR

I'm a USA Today bestselling romance author who's passionate about ***fast-paced, emotion-filled*** contemporary romantic suspense and science fiction romance. I love writing about people overcoming unbeatable odds and achieving seemingly impossible goals. I like to believe it's possible for all of us to do the same.

I live in Australia with my own personal hero and two very busy, always-on-the-move sons.

For release dates, behind-the-scenes info, free books, and other fun stuff, sign up for the latest news here:

Website: www.annahackett.com

www.ingramcontent.com/pod-product-compliance
Lightning Source LLC
Chambersburg PA
CBHW030254200626
46816CB00002BA/642